The Story of Her Holding an Orange

MILOS BOGETIC

The Story of Her Holding an Orange

Copyright © 2013 by Milos Bogetic

Published by Inaaace Press.

Printed in the United States of America.

ISBN: 0615776108

ISBN-13: 978-0615776101

*For my brother Mijo, who introduced me to horror way
before the horror found me.*

Special thanks to those whose generosity made this

publication possible-

Megan Simpson

Shrina Patel

JPS

Srdjan Popovic

Seth Numburg

Collette Nadeau

Anthony Foglia

Aaron Rankin

Rebekah Money

NoSleep Community

Introduction

Hi. I don't want to bore you with a classic introduction, so let's get straight to the point.

I am a logical man. I also like to believe that I'm somewhat intelligent. When curtains in my room move at night, I assume it's the wind and not a ghost. I suppose my point is that I always look for a rational explanation for everything. What you're about to read, however, I have no explanation for. I won't tell you that the things that happened to me were supernatural. But I will say that my mind hasn't been able to fully rationalize the events that happened to me.

One more thing I want to address. I don't think that this book meets the traditional standards of novel length or style. Shit, I probably break every rule of proper writing. I curse, I lack form, I start sentences with words I shouldn't start sentences with, and, well, I just write the way I speak.

I was advised to expand on my story, but I refused because, honestly, I felt like that would be unfair to you. You didn't buy this to read artistic, multi-paragraph descriptions of simple events. You got this so you can read about what happened to me, told from my perspective. Your Kindles, iPads, and bookshelves are already overflowing with books that speak to you in beautiful language. This writing is filled with curses and simple storytelling.

But (Rule Number 1 – Never start your sentence with *but*) enough with the introductory stuff. I'll let you get to what actually happened.

Good luck.

1

How I Met Rose

In June of '92, when the first bullet was shot in Bosnia, marking the beginning of an awful fucking war, I was in Montenegro. My parents had some inkling of the shit that was about to go down and took my brother and me away just in time.

Adjusting to a new life didn't come easy to any of us. I suppose I had it the best; I was still young, and adapting to the new school and new friends wasn't hard. My parents and older brother had a much tougher time, however. I remember when my mom got the job - her first job since we had moved. We were all as happy as could be. This not only meant that our financial situation would improve, but also that she would be able to blend into the new society and hopefully make friends.

Man, I wish she didn't get that job.

My mother's new job was working as an advisor to the president of the Montenegrin Academy of Arts and Sciences. This was basically just a fancy name for an institution that deals with pushing culture into society. Mom enjoyed the work and had made some really good friends over the decade she worked there.

About ten years into working at this place, she made friends with a woman named Rose. It was strange to me, really; my mother was never one to make friends quickly, yet as soon as Rose started working at the academy, they became the best of friends. They spent an awful lot of time together. Every few days, Rose would stop by our house for a cup of coffee and some fresh gossip, a tradition native to all the Balkan countries.

I, personally, really liked Rose. I could tell you it was her personality or humor that made me look at her favorably, but no. No, the woman was just hot, plain and simple. Rose was about 5'6", slender, and very pale. She had long black hair with black eyes that I'd get lost in, and her trademark bright red lipstick made her already white teeth gleam. Overall, she was a very captivating individual. I never really got to speak with her much, not that I even wanted to. She was a frequent visitor in my fantasies (hey, I was a puberty-stricken kid at the time), and I liked leaving it at that.

One day, when I was about seventeen, Rose came to our house for the usual routine of Turkish coffee and the latest gossip. I remembered being bored out of my mind at the time - in Montenegro, we used to have limits on Internet usage, and I would burn through mine within days.

Internetless (my word, ©), I decided to join Rose and Mom at the balcony and hear what was new in town. About twenty minutes into a conversation that was nearly unbearably boring for a teenager, Mom got up.

"I almost forgot," she said, "I baked a cake yesterday! Rose, you must have a piece."

"Well, alright, but just a little one. I gotta watch the figure, you know," Rose responded, looking at me. Maybe she expected me to say she didn't need to worry about losing weight, I don't know.

As my mom left the balcony, an awkward silence took over. I stared at the ground, my brain working in overdrive, trying to think of a topic that would break this uncomfortable monotony. I looked over to Rose and noticed her smiling. This was strange since I hadn't said a word to her since my mom left us alone. Then she turned to me. I immediately felt that something was... off.

"You ready?" is what I *think* she said. I can't be sure because she said it in a voice so quiet, it was nearly impossible to hear.

"Excuse me?" I asked.

Rose tilted her head to the left. Her motions became extremely slow, almost as if she had suddenly become a puppet. Her smile had widened into an eerie Cheshire Cat grin.

"You ready to take it now?" she asked. Her voice had changed and reminded me of a very young girl's. She spoke through her teeth, never opening her mouth.

"What?" I asked, starting to feel uncomfortable.

"You ready?" she asked again, as if I was supposed to know what the fuck she was talking about. She still spoke in that eight-year-old voice, never opening her mouth, while her head tilted in an unnatural angle.

"Look, I don't know what you're talking abo—"

She cut me off. "It's time to take it now," she said, pulling out her purse from under the table. "It really is."

Then she took an orange out of her bag. That's all she did. She didn't offer it to me; she didn't eat it herself, or say anything else. She just held it there.

At that point, as I imagine any kid would, I was getting scared as fuck. I was absolutely speechless at this sudden transformation of a grown woman into some sort of a puppet-child with an orange. Luckily, I heard the balcony door open and my mom walked in.

"Who's ready for some cake?" she asked cheerfully, breaking the tension in the air.

Just like that, Rose switched back to normal. She tucked the orange back into her purse, cocked her head back into a natural human position, and smiled a normal human smile.

"Oh, that looks wonderful, what did you put in it?" Rose asked in her own adult voice, looking at the piece of cake my mom put in front of her.

I got up, confused and scared, and walked out.

"You're not going to have any cake, Milos?" Rose asked, right before I was about to close the door.

I looked at her right in the eyes. Man, I swear I saw something unnatural in them, but I just can't define it properly. It was a look that was fully aware of the shit that had happened just a moment ago. A look of confidence. A look that told me this story wasn't over; rather, it had just begun.

"No, I'm ok," I said, shutting the door.

I spent the rest of the day in my room avoiding any further contact with Rose.

That night, I had trouble sleeping. Every time I'd try to doze off, that childish, unnatural voice would pop into my head.

"*It's time to take it now.*"

I was covered in goosebumps, but still sweating under the blanket. Every few minutes, I'd look at my window. My room was on the first floor and the window was pretty low, probably only 5 feet above the ground, making it very easy for anyone to peek through. Just as I was about to convince myself that I was overreacting, I looked into the window one final time.

And there she was. Standing at the fucking window.

The brightness of the moonlight only added to the glow of Rose's pale skin, making her look unnaturally white. Her red lipstick was excessively bright, which in turn accented her pearly white teeth. The woman just stood at the window, looking at me, her head tilted, and smiling.

You know how you sometimes think of hypothetical situations and what you'd do in them? Like if a shooter walks into a movie theater, where you'd run, where you'd hide, etc.? I always did that in my room. And in every hypothetical I could think of, I had an escape plan. Yet, when this strange, child-like puppet woman showed up at my window, I was motionless with fear. My mouth immediately went dry, and chills ran down my spine (and they are again as I'm typing this). After what seemed like an absolute eternity but was probably only a minute or two, I decided that I had to do something. I slowly removed the blanket and stood up.

Rose remained motionless, other than her smile getting wider. I suppose me getting up was exactly what she wanted. Slowly and gingerly, almost as if I expected her to break through the window if I moved too quickly, I started walking towards her. And with every step I'd make, her head would turn to follow me. Every motion of hers was so mechanic, so... unnatural. It really is difficult to convey the absurdity of that situation. Here I was, a teenage boy in his room late at night, looking at a strange pale woman who was standing outside the window and smiling.

I was about to run out of my room and scream for my parents, but knowing how tense and easily excitable they are, I chose to stay quiet for the time being. I guess I didn't want to make a huge fuss if Rose was just going to go right back to normal again. For fuck knows what reason, I decided to talk to her. There had to be a rational explanation for this irrational behavior, right? At worst, she was mentally ill. At best... Well, I don't know what the best scenario would've been. Probably one of my fantasies coming true, but trust me - standing in my room that night, wet dreams were the last thing on my mind.

I took a slow step towards the window, and stopped immediately when she moved. She slowly put a hand into her black leather purse and pulled an orange out of it. Again, every motion was terribly inhuman, almost robotic. The urge to run away shot through my body again, and I could feel the blood pumping through the big veins in my neck. Thinking that, if push came to shove, I could easily fight this fragile-looking woman off, I walked towards her again.

The closer I got, the wider her smile became. I wish I had a picture of that scene that night... Me, standing in front of a window in my boxers and a t-shirt, and outside, a strange woman holding an orange. My window was made of thick glass, so I had to push the window up if I wanted to talk to her. I opened the window maybe ten inches, and stopped. I looked at her. That was enough for her to hear me, yet not enough for her to come in.

"What the fuck are you doing?" I whispered, not wanting my parents to hear. I have no idea why I didn't want them seeing this lunatic at my window.

Rose didn't answer. Instead, she started bending. Bending towards the opening. I made a quick step back just as she managed to push her head through the hole.

"You ready to take it now?" she asked in her child-voice. I thought that her voice had been scary at the balcony, but hearing it in the dead of the night gave me an all-new wave of shivers.

As she spoke, her right hand snaked its way through the window. In it was the orange.

Terrified by the increasing horror of this absurd situation, I decided to run.

"Dad! Dad!" I screamed, running through the hallway and towards my parents' room.

By the time I got to the master bedroom, they were both already on their feet.

"What the fuck is going on?!" my dad demanded.

All I could muster through my shaking jaw was, "Rose... Window."

While my dad went to the closet to get his pants and perhaps some sort of weapon, I ran back to my room. I wanted Rose to be there so bad. You know how, in those horror movies, the main character screams for help, and when the help finally comes, the monster is always gone? Well, when I made it back to the room, I was still able to see Rose. She was getting away, however. I could see her right next to our house, in our neighbor's back yard that was equipped with one of those motion-activated lights. Rose set the sensor off, and the yard lit up just enough for me to watch her disappear behind the corner of a neighbor's house. When my father ran into my room, she was gone. I wanted her to be there so bad. I wanted to tell them what was happening. Instead, all I got from my dad was an angry "you and your fucking imagination" as he left my room. Needless to say, I got exactly zero hours of sleep that night.

Nothing happened for the next two months or so. During the few days after the incident, I was incredibly tense and would be set off by even the smallest sound coming from outside my window. Rose did come visit my mom for their standard gossip evenings, but I would never be around. Fuck that. Tuesday and Thursday afternoons were reserved for Rose's visits, and I would come up with different excuses not to be there.

Since I successfully avoided Rose and she never stalked me again, I started to forget about the incident. As with every other teenager in the world, I had an attention span of a butterfly, and there just wasn't enough room in my mind for that woman.

2

She's Back

I was sitting in my room, browsing whatever website was popular at the time. I'd become pretty hungry, and as does every lazy child, I yelled for my mom to make me a sandwich. She didn't answer. I realized that I wasn't sure if she was even home, so I had to get my lazy ass up and make my own food. Our kitchen is connected to the living room but is set up in such a way that you can't see the room unless you're in the middle of the dining area.

As soon as I entered the kitchen, I froze. In the middle of the table sat an orange. Nothing else, just one solitary orange. Flashes of Rose's pale face at my window came back, and I swear I could feel the air becoming colder around me. I stared motionless for a few seconds before snapping myself out of it.

It's a piece of fruit in the kitchen, man, chill out, I thought, smirking at my own cowardice.

I started making my sandwich, but no matter how much I told myself it was just an orange on the table, the unsettled feeling in my stomach wouldn't go away. *Fuck it,* I thought, *I'll put it away.* I stepped into the kitchen, looked up - and saw Rose.

"You will have to take it soon, you know," she said, tilting her head to the left, smiling as widely as humanly possible. She looked exactly the same as that fucking night two months ago: long white dress of almost the same bright shade as her skin with dark black hair falling down her shoulders. Her lipstick looked to be an even brighter red than before, which only amplified the effect of her nearly blinding teeth. Once again, she spoke in a voice of a little girl.

There she was, a woman who had abused my sanity months ago, standing in my living room, tilting her head, speaking in a voice of a child. And then - and fucking then - she put her hand in her purse and took out an orange. She pulled it out slowly, her motions resembling those more of a disturbed robot than an actual human.

"This is for you," she said.

My mind was racing. I had no fucking clue what to do. And just as my defensive instincts were about to kick in, either to attack this crazy cunt or run away from her, my mom walked in. I know it didn't really happen that way, but it seemed as if my mother brought the light back into the room with her. The whole horror of the situation diffused as fast as it began, at least for the moment. Rose quickly put the orange back into her purse, straightening her neck back into a normal position.

"Rose and I are going for a walk, ok?" my mom asked. I didn't answer. As they left the room, Rose turned around and gave me another one of her creepy fucking smiles.

I waited for both of my parents to come home that night so I could tell them the truth. I realized that the burden of proof was solely on me, but I had to do it. When my mother and father finally came home, I sat down and started telling them the entire story. I told them about the balcony incident. I told them that Rose was really at the window that night and that I wasn't imagining things. I said that she stood in the living room and harassed me while my mom was getting ready for the walk. I told them everything, but I could tell that they believed absolutely none of it. They listened to me, yes, but after I was finished, they said nothing. As soon as I asked what they thought was going on, my dad called my older brother to come in and yelled at him for making me watch horror movies. My mom got up and started making dinner. And just like that, my whole story was forgotten by everyone but me. And Rose.

About three months passed, and Rose hadn't paid me another visit. I had trouble forgetting about her, though; she'd often come to visit my mom, and of course, she acted normal in front of my family. By that time, I had decided that Rose had mental issues and was most likely suffering from a multiple personality disorder or something similar. My theory was that, for some reason, I triggered one of those individuals inside her head. I avoided any conversation with her since the last thing in the world I wanted was to deal with a crazy child-mimicking lady offering me a fucking orange.

Four months after the last living room incident, my brother's birthday came up. Every year, he'd organize a huge party at our house. We were good, trustworthy kids, so our parents would go away for the night, and my brother and I would celebrate it with his friends and no adults. The party started off really promising; there were about fifty people at our house and it wasn't even 10pm. We were all having so much fun; the music was good, the food and drinks were plentiful, and the atmosphere was absolutely amazing. Until about midnight, when the doorbell rang.

When I saw her standing at the front door, I nearly dropped my drink. Luckily, she hadn't noticed me yet in the crowd. I ran to my brother.

"Mijo!" I hissed, grabbing his arm, "Mijo, what the fuck is Rose doing here?"

"What are you talking about?" he asked, looking as surprised as I was. Then he looked over to the door and saw her. "Oh, for fuck's sake. Did Mom and Dad have her come to spy on us?"

"I don't think so... man, go tell her to fuck off. Please."

My brother could see how unsettled I was. It was then that he probably realized I was telling the truth this whole time.

"Hold on, are you serious? She actually did stalk you?" Mijo asked, looking intrigued.

"That's what I've been trying to tell you people! That woman is batshit crazy, man."

Mijo winked at me. "I got you," he said and walked over to the door. Rose was just standing there, smiling and scoping the crowd. I watched them talking for a good five minutes, wondering why the conversation was taking so long. Then my brother moved to the side, letting Rose into the house. He came over to me, carrying a box.

"What the fuck are you doing, why'd you let her in?" I nearly yelled at him.

"Look, she said she was nearby and heard it was my birthday, so she brought me a gift, see?" Mijo said, opening the box he got from Rose. It was an mp3 player. "And, it's exactly the one I wanted!"

"Dude," I said while battling the temptation to knock the gift out of his hands, "did you forget what I just told you? She is fucking crazy; she's here for me."

"Look, I don't know what is going on between you two, but I can't kick Mom's friend out of our house when she brought me a gift. You work it out with her. Besides, there are like 75 people here. You're safe." Mijo walked away into the crowd, and I stood there, surrounded by people, feeling lonelier than ever.

I spent most of the party sitting in the corner, looking out for Rose. I saw her here and there, like when she went to get a drink or when she talked to some of my brother's friends. I suppose she quickly became the highlight of the party, and I could see why; she was a hot, mature lady who hung out with young people. Guys were all over her, and girls loved her. I fucking hated it. It was killing me that I was alone in my own house full of friends. I couldn't take it anymore, so I walked outside. Sitting in the dark in my front yard, I half expected her to pop outside into the blackness and offer me an orange. Who knows, maybe I even *wanted* her to do it. That way, I could draw other people's attention and then all 75 people could see how disturbed this woman was.

Fortunately or unfortunately, depending how you look at it, she didn't come. The party started winding down around 3am, and by 3:30, most people were gone. When I walked back into the house, the final group, including Rose, was getting ready to leave.

"Milos, I haven't seen much of you tonight," Rose said while putting her coat on. "Is everything ok with you?"

I didn't answer. I just stood there, looking her straight in the eyes, almost as if I wanted to send her a message saying, "Fuck you, bitch, you're not intimidating me."

"Um, he's been acting strange all night, don't pay him any mind," said my brother while helping Rose with her coat, "and thanks so much for the gift; it's exactly the one I wanted."

"Oh, you're most welcome, Mijo," she said. As she walked out of the house, she turned around, looked at me, and said, "And I'll see you soon, Milos." Her creepy fucking grin was the last thing I saw before she shut the door.

"Did you see that?" I asked my brother.

"See what?"

"You didn't think that was weird at all?" I asked, almost begging for some sort of confirmation that I wasn't the one going crazy.

"Dude, you need to chill out with this whole Rose thing. She was awesome tonight. And she didn't harass you, did she?"

I hung my head in defeat. "No," I admitted.

"See? It's all good. Now, let's get some sleep; we gotta get up early and clean this place before Mom and Dad come back."

I slowly walked to my room, feeling the frustration build inside me. I felt so helpless. Not even my own family would believe a word I said. I walked into my room and collapsed on the soft bed. I was so tired that I fell asleep immediately, without even taking my clothes off. At some point during the night, I got really cold, so I rolled under the blankets without really waking up. I was all set to go right back to sleep when I felt something cold and wet underneath me.

"What the fuck…?" I said out loud. I jumped and flipped the light switch.

In my bed was a crushed orange.

Tears started pouring down my cheeks. At that moment, I realized that there was no escape for me. I had nowhere to run, and Rose's persistence was so convincing that I had no doubt she'd eventually get what she wanted.

I stood looking at that crushed piece of fruit for a good ten minutes. I wanted to look through the window, but I was afraid of what I'd see. I walked over to my brother's room.

"Mijo," I said, shaking him. "Mijo, wake up. There's an orange in my bed."

"What?" he asked, sounding angry that I woke him up. "What's happening?"

"Rose left an orange in my bed, man."

"Go back to fucking bed. I swear, you and your fucking oranges," said my brother as he turned around and went back to sleep.

That was when I knew that this would be a journey that I'd have to take alone. Rose was far too good to give away her monstrous nature in front of others. What bothered me the most was that she harassed me in the subtlest of ways. On the balcony, she acted crazy right until my mom walked in, then switched back to normal. She stood at my bedroom window and got away right before my dad was able to spot her. In the living room, she was a child-puppet who turned into a normal adult only in my mother's presence. And finally, she was the center of my brother's party but had managed to leave a message strong enough to make me cry, yet not big enough to make my brother think anything strange was happening. She always danced around the edge of being discovered but was too good (or experienced) to actually reveal her true self. And that is what was driving me insane.

3

The Final Incident
and
Farewell Rose

One full year had passed since the first time Rose had offered me the orange. While I was always on the lookout for her to show up at my window, I had other things on my mind. Since I was making a name for myself in the basketball world, many American colleges had heard of me and started the recruiting process. Wanting the degree, but also secretly wanting to get away from the discomfort of always having to have my guard up, I decided to head to the U.S. After much debating, I chose Penn State University as my school. I had about four weeks to get ready for my American adventure, so I headed over to a basketball camp in a city some 40 miles away from home.

Training and mental preparation went according to plan. Multiple workouts a day and studying for the SAT in my hotel room was my routine for weeks. Three days before the end of the camp, my roommate was injured in practice and his parents came and took him home, so I had a whole room to myself. I didn't mind this at all since I had to study and I enjoyed peace and quiet.

The last day of camp, I decided to take a break from both studying and working out. My hotel was only a ten-minute walk from the beach, so I spent the whole day laying in the sun and swimming. I got back to my room, took a shower, and collapsed in bed, exhausted. You know how sometimes when you're too tired, you can't sleep? Well, after a good hour of turning and flipping in bed, I decided to go out to the balcony and get some fresh air. I opened the door and sat on one of the chairs. The view overlooking the ocean was beautiful, and I started getting sleepy again.

"It is really time to take it now."

I nearly shat myself. I mean, it'd been a while since I'd heard that voice, but something like that stays with you forever. That childish, mechanical tone. I turned to the right. Rose was standing on the balcony rail. Mind you, she wasn't sitting at the balcony table nor was she standing in a natural position; no, she was standing *on* the balcony rail. This probably wouldn't be as shocking if the floor we were on wasn't some fifty feet above the ground. To make things more absurd, she was holding an orange.

Try to imagine it. Go ahead, just try for a second. You're alone in your hotel room. You walk outside on the balcony at maybe 4am. Suddenly, you hear a child's voice say something to you. You look to your right and see a grown woman standing on the rail of a third floor balcony, holding an orange, telling you that it is "time to take it."

Two different kinds of fear overcame my suddenly sobered up mind. First, I was obviously afraid of this fucking lunatic standing on the balcony next to me. Second, I was terrified that she may try to jump. Only a few feet separated our balconies, and such a jump would be entirely possible, but if she didn't make it, I was afraid I'd somehow be blamed for it. I had no idea what to do.

"It really is time, you know. That's the only way to transfer," she whispered in that goddamn child-like voice without ever opening the teeth that looked even whiter in the dark of night. I remember the orange looked dark, almost rotten, and certainly not as "orange" as the first time she took it out.

"What the fuck do you want from me?!" I screamed at her. I screamed because of all the frustration that had been building up since the day she started the orange horror. I screamed because I wanted someone to hear and come to witness the madness this woman was putting me through.

"I only want you to take it," she said, widening her grin to nearly inhuman proportions. Her teeth remained clenched, and her head tilted to the left.

"Fuck you, you crazy bitch," I said after realizing that no witnesses were going to show up this late at night. I opened the door and walked into my room. As I shut the door, I heard, "You will take it," from the outside. I spent the rest of the night keeping an eye on the terrace, but she never came. I wasn't brave enough to check if she was still standing on the fence of the neighboring balcony. Morning couldn't have come soon enough. Right as the first sunrays hit my window, I carried my bag out to the reception desk and waited for my father to pick me up. I decided not to say anything about this incident because I was sure I would, yet again, be blamed for an over-active imagination.

I was leaving the continent in a day. The night before the trip, my mom made me call my grandmother in Bosnia and say goodbye to her. We talked for a long time, and she gave me all the pieces of advice you'd expect your grandma to give. Her instructions ranged from "Americans are crazy, be careful" to "find a good girl and get married so I can see my great-grandkids before I die." Towards the end of the conversation, though, she noticed there was something wrong with me.

"You're being awfully quiet, Milos?" she asked.

"Eh, it's nothing, grandma. It's all going to be all right tomorrow when I leave."

"What is it?" she persisted.

"Well, you won't believe me anyway," I sighed.

"Try me."

"Okay, okay. Here comes the product of my wild imagination, as Dad calls it. So, there's this woman, Mom's friend, right? She comes over all the time, but whenever we're left alone, she acts strange. I mean, really strange."

"Strange, how?" asked my grandmother, sounding quite interested.

"Strange as in she talks in a child's voice, her motions are mechanical, and... I don't know, Grandma, there's just something wrong about her.

About a good minute of silence came after that last sentence.

"You still there?" I asked, checking to see if the line had disconnected.

"Listen, Milos. You'll be all right. Tomorrow, you leave for America. Whatever that woman was doing to you will stop," my grandma said, sounding energetic. I wasn't sure if the fire in her words was coming from excitement because she believed me, or because she wanted to end the conversation soon.

"So... you believe me?" I asked, hoping that at least one adult would acknowledge my misery.

"Yes."

I wasn't sure if I got an affirmative answer because she wanted to get rid of me or she actually believed me, but it was good enough. We said our goodbyes, and I hung up and continued packing. The next day, I was going to start a new life far away from all the supernatural, fruit-bearing crazy people. It would be fine.

I've never been more wrong in my life.

4

The Land of Opportunity

Coming to America was a life-changing experience on many levels. My world had completely changed; none of my family was close by, and I had to experience an entirely new culture all by myself. All of the difficulties I'd encountered, however, were offset by the peace I found. I was no longer stalked by a woman who wanted me to take her orange. Sure, for the first few months after my arrival, I kept an eye out for Rose. I was sure she didn't follow me this far, but I wasn't going to relax just yet. After all, she had proved to be insane on many occasions before.

Every time I'd speak to my parents over Skype, I'd sneak in a question about Rose just to make sure she was still in Europe. As time passed, my mom mentioned that she was seeing less and less of Rose for some reason she couldn't understand. I assumed it was because I was no longer in the house, but I said nothing.

Seven wonderful years passed since the first day I landed in the home of the brave, and it had been one hell of a ride; I'd received two degrees and had gotten to experience many amazing cities and everything that America had to offer. On top of it all, I met a wonderful girl who soon became my girlfriend. In a nutshell, life was good, man. My girlfriend Trish and I moved to a small town in Cape Cod to spend the summer. It was one of the best summers in my life, all the way up until September 21st.

I'm a massive technology geek, and some of you would probably label me an Apple fanboy. What can I say? I fucking love their products. So, September 21st - the release day of the much-anticipated, new and improved iPhone 5. The town we lived in was about a two-hour drive from Boston, where the closest Apple store was located, so I rented a car and got there really early. Even though I was in front of the store way before the sun even came up, I was about 15th in line. About four hours into the wait, the main door opened and the line started to move slowly. When I got close to the entrance, I looked to my right and instantly froze. People ran into my back, and I could hear some curses, but that was all white noise to me at the moment.

Across the street stood Rose.

There was no doubt it was her: white dress with red shoes, long black hair with pale skin, and a red lipstick so bright, you could see it from a block away. In her hand, she held an orange. A million and one things raced through my mind. Was it really her? How the fuck did she find me? What was going to happen now; am I back into my old life?

Someone behind me couldn't take my pondering anymore and pushed me. I was still frozen in shock and fell down, never taking my eyes off of her. Rose dropped the orange and walked away, disappearing behind the nearby corner. I gathered myself and got up. Thinking that I may have been just making this shit up, I walked into the store. Unfortunately, there were already no phones left, so I decided to walk across the street and see if I could see something to confirm what I had hoped was a hallucination.

And there it was. There it fucking was. In the spot where I had thought I saw Rose standing was now an extremely rotten, squished orange. A flood of emotions overcame me, and I broke down and started crying, right in the middle of Boylston Street in Boston.

After a few minutes, I dragged myself into a nearby Starbucks. I spent the next few hours drinking gallons of hot tea and contemplating what was happening. I simply couldn't believe that she had found me. I mean, sure, me being in America was no secret; every one of my friends and family knew that I was here, and there's always Facebook. But even if she knew that I lived in the U.S., even if she knew my fucking address, how, or rather, *why* would she travel across the planet? Just so I can take that fucking piece of rotten fruit? I was baffled at these events. I decided to go back home and hope that Rose wouldn't find out where I lived. I decided not to tell Trish anything. Nobody believed me before this, and there was no reason she would, either. And even if she did, all my story would do is terrify her, which would be pointless. Plus, there was always an off chance that I just imagined Rose being there, and the orange in the street was only a freakish coincidence.

It took me two days to convince myself that I couldn't have possibly seen Rose from that far away. That it was some random lady who just resembled her. That the orange was a fluke of the universe that had decided to fuck with me. Trish did suspect that something was wrong with me, but I refused to open up. Then, four days later, a letter came in the mail. Receiving a letter isn't strange in itself since I get a lot of mail. Sorting through the endless envelopes offering credit cards and coupons, I came upon a strange looking one. This particular envelope had no return address but sure as hell had my name on it.

Opening it made my worst nightmare come true. Inside of it was a Polaroid picture. A picture of me. A picture of me standing in front of the Apple store that Friday, September 21st. The photograph was taken by someone behind me. The most shocking part was that the picture was snapped in exactly the same moment I spotted Rose; I could tell because there was a look of complete horror on my face. On the back of the Polaroid was written with a black pen:

YOU TAKE IT, NOW

I dropped the picture and started crying like a little baby. I am a grown man, and I sobbed like an infant that just entered this cold world. When Trish walked into our room, I was in a fetal position with my shirt and pillow soaked with tears of horror. She immediately assumed someone in my family had died, since she had never seen me cry before.

"Oh god... babe. Babe, what's the matter? Is it someone from back home?" she asked, giving me the strongest hug I ever got from her.

I couldn't bring myself to speak for another ten minutes or so. Trish just sat next to me, hugging me and waiting to hear what it was that brought her boyfriend to such tears. When I finally calmed down, I sat up, grabbed her hand, and started as gently as I could.

"Babe, what you're about to hear... I can't really explain it. But I need you to trust me."

"Of course I will."

And just like that, everything got a little better. Not much, but just a little. Sure, my life and possibly hers was about to go to shit, but man, *finally* someone was ready to believe me. And I was sure having seen me absolutely devastated a minute ago would lend credibility to my story. I spent the next few minutes telling the story, leaving most of the details out as I just wanted her to get an idea of what I'd been going through. She just sat there, saying nothing, looking at me with utmost fascination.

"...and that's basically it," I finished, looking into her eyes, hoping I wouldn't see that *"I'm dating a lunatic"* look. But she didn't say anything. She kept looking at me with her jaw hanging a little, presumably out of shock.

"Babe, I know it's a lot to handle, but please believe me..." I pleaded with her.

"That woman..." she murmured finally.

"Rose, yes," I answered.

"Did she... did she offer you an orange?"

5

Trish's Story

My girlfriend was born in Kenya, Africa, but her family moved to Canada when she was three. Trish is Indian, if that matters at all. I met her exactly two years ago in a Cape Cod town called Provincetown. She was a flight attendant for Air Canada at the time, and had come to visit the place with a few friends at the same time I was spending my summer there.

There was only one real club to go out to in the whole town, and after it closed at 2am, people would gather on benches in front of it and just hang out. I was on the street with my brother and best friend, and we were just standing and chatting. At one point, we were approached by an older gentleman who appeared to be intoxicated. Things became hilarious when he started openly hitting on me. Even after I'd told him multiple times that I was not interested in his increasingly forward offers, he became even pushier. Just as I was about to leave and go home, letting this man ruin my so far perfect night, I heard a female voice from the benches.

"Hey, baby, what're you doing?"

I turned around and saw Trish. She was sitting on the bench with two other people. I've never met her before, so I wasn't sure if she was actually talking to me.

"Well, are you going to sit with me or what?" she asked, looking straight into my eyes. I realized that she was trying to save me from the man.

"Excuse me," I said, walking towards Trish, "my fiancé is calling me."

The man wouldn't buy the story, and he came after me. I sat next to Trish.

"Is he really your fiancé?" the man asked.

"Yep," she answered with confidence.

"Prove it."

That was the first time Trish and I kissed. The man left us alone shortly after that. Trish and I have been together ever since, and I still owe her for saving me that day.

There are so many things that are fascinating about Trish's life, but none more so than the fact that she knew about Rose.

∞∞∞∞∞∞∞∞∞∞∞∞∞∞∞∞∞

"Did she offer me an orange? How the hell did you know?" I asked, feeling ill from this second shock of the day.

"She - I saw her before," was all Trish managed to say before she broke down crying.

Trish held on tight to me, and we spent the next hour or so in complete silence. I knew that we were both emotionally drained, but I just had to find out how she knew about Rose.

"Rose... How'd you know about her?"

"I didn't know her name was Rose... but I have met her a few times."

This is Trish's story.

∞∞∞∞∞∞∞∞∞∞∞∞∞∞∞∞∞∞

The first encounter with Rose that my girlfriend remembers was on a plane. Trish was working one of those short-distance flights. She remembers noticing Rose before even interacting with her. Trish says that she saw this woman, attractive but extremely pale, sitting in the economy class and grinning as wide as she could. She had no earphones nor any other devices or books that could make her smile, so it was a strange thing to do, but Trish brushed it off. When she came up to Rose to offer her a drink and complimentary peanuts, the damn woman only widened her smile, not answering.

"Excuse me, ma'am, do you speak English? Français?"

"I have something for you," Rose answered in perfect English. What was troubling, though, was that she spoke with a voice that seemed like it belonged to a young girl rather than an adult woman.

Now, Trish has seen some shit during her flying career. She's dealt with them all: flirters, complainers, troublemakers, love makers, you name it. Hearing a woman speak with a childish voice was strange, but not any stranger than a man from the week before who started screaming mid-flight about someone standing on the wing of a plane. Trish's strategy was to always play along and entertain such people to the extent of her powers and comfort.

"Oh yeah? And what would that be?" she responded to Rose with a smile on her face.

"Don't patronize me, you little bitch," Rose fired back. She spoke very quickly, without her jaw ever opening, and somehow maintained that fucking smile on her face the entire time.

This was a red flag for Trish, who always walked away from confrontations with aggressive passengers unless actual physical contact took place, in which case the rest of the crew and Air Marshal would take over.

"Alright, well, you have a wonderful rest of the flight, ma'am, ok?" Trish responded, forcing herself to smile.

"I have this for you," Rose said, pulling out an orange from behind her back. Again, she never opened her mouth, yet she managed to speak clearly. Oddly, her voice still sounded like that of a little girl.

"No, thanks," said Trish, deciding to call it a day with the crazy lady.

"Oh, but you should. You really should."

"No," Trish said firmly, walking away.

"One day, then," Rose whispered.

And that's that. Trish gave her a "fuck off" look and stayed away from Rose's section for the rest of the flight. When they landed, Trish made sure she was nowhere near the exit while people left so she wouldn't have to deal with this strange woman.

My girlfriend went home that night. When her mom asked her how the flight went, Trish responded, "Good, other than one crazy lady. Why can't I ever get a normal flight?"

"What crazy lady?" asked her mom.

So, Trish started telling her about Rose. By the time she mentioned the orange, her mom started crying. Needless to say, it was story time.

Apparently, when Trish was just a baby in Kenya, she would often wake her parents up by crying loudly. When her mom and dad would come into the room, there would be an orange in Trish's crib. The problem was, all the doors and windows were always locked. Her dad searched the house every time an incident like this happened, but he could never find any evidence of a break-in. When the orange incidents started becoming more scary than mysterious, Trish's parents installed security cameras in their house. This seemed to eliminate the issue almost instantly.

However, on Trish's third birthday, the final incident happened. When her parents walked into her room that morning, they saw an orange lying on her chest. Naturally, they went to check the security cameras, and sure enough, Rose was there. They could clearly see Rose walking in the house, as if she owned the key to it. She then proceeded to walk to Trish's room. Her mom said that, even though it was dark inside the house, you could see how pale the woman was. She was smiling. When Rose walked into the baby's room, she gently placed the orange on Trish's chest and just stood there. For a good hour. Just stood there, rocking back and forth and looking at the baby, with her head tilted to the left. When Trish's dad got up to go to the bathroom around 4am, Rose stopped the staring and rocking thing and simply walked away. She didn't appear to be at all worried that she'd be caught.

The first thing Trish's family did was call the police, but knowing the effectiveness of the Kenyan police, they hardly felt comforted. Although the officers promised to do an extensive investigation on these break-ins, Trish's dad knew he had to do something else. Hiring 24/7 security wasn't an option because of their financial situation at the time. Trish's mother's side of the family already lived in Canada and had been pressuring her parents to move there, so these events were the final push for them.

Trish was devastated by her mom's story. Lost and scared, she spent the next few days in her room, thinking about what could possibly be the reason for this woman to stalk her. Her parents had absolutely no idea why these things were happening.

But by a few days later, Trish had made herself believe that it was all some sort of fucked up coincidence. She felt safe at home, and nothing further happened, so she decided to leave this absurdity behind and move on with her life. She lived in peace for two years, until she met Rose again.

Trish was, and still is, an avid surfer. Surfing and flying are her two main passions in life. In 2010, she decided to take a vacation and go to Nicaragua, where she'd spend the summer riding waves. This trip had been her dream ever since she got her first surfboard.

She spent most of the summer having the time of her life. She was surrounded by great friends, she'd spend days surfing and tanning, you know, she lived the good life. And just when she started wondering if she had come close to perfect happiness, Rose came back.

Once a week, Trish and her friends would throw a nighttime beach party that involved drinking, grilling, and of course, surfing. It was her favorite part of the summer; they would all sit around the fire, drink whatever liquor or beer they had, and cook some good food. Then, they'd jump on their boards and ride the ocean for an hour or two. This particular night, when everyone was ready to jump in the water, Trish felt ill. She assumed that she either ate something bad or that the cheap vodka was finally getting to her. She told everyone to go ahead and that she'd join soon.

Lying by the fire in the soft, comfortable sand, Trish started dozing off. When the fire started dying down, she sat up and saw a man sitting next to her. Many people would often join these parties, so that wasn't strange. What *was* strange was that the man wore a suit. He sat very close to Trish, causing her to immediately sober up. She noticed he didn't wear any shoes and that his whole outfit, except for the white dress shirt, was black. He even wore one of those old-school top hats. The entire outfit was completely inappropriate for both the beach and the entire climate of tropical Nicaragua.

"Did you sleep well, Trish?" he asked her, smiling and looking at the dying fire.

"Yes… Do I know you?"

"Oh, no, I don't believe you do, Trish," the man responded, turning towards her. She noticed that he looked extremely old and young at the same time, as strange as that sounds. His face had clearly been through decades and decades of life, but his eyes... his eyes seemed as young as an infant's, with an unnatural shine and energy hiding in them.

"Then how do you know my name?" she asked, slowly moving away from the man.

"You know, Trish," the man said, brushing off the sand from his coat sleeves, "you should really take it."

Trish froze instantly. Not only was there a strange man in a black suit sitting next to her on the beach, but he also knew her name... and it seemed that he knew more than that.

"Take... take it?" Trish managed to whisper, not wanting to hear the answer.

"Yes, take it," the man responded, pointing to a spot in the distance ahead. Trish looked to where he pointed and a wave of shivers ran down her spine. Out of the dark in front of them emerged Rose. She walked slowly, almost mechanically. She was smiling and tilting her head to the left, and in her hand was an orange.

"You're ready," said the man, standing up and brushing the remaining sand off of his suit, "you really are. Transfer will be complete." Rose walked up to him and they just stood there, looking at a stunned Trish.

She always has tremendous trouble talking about this event because this was the first time she felt truly unsafe. The first time she had encountered Rose, she was a baby and she didn't remember anything. The second time, well, she was on a plane surrounded by people. This time, she was sitting on a beach alone, and Rose now had someone else with her. With her extremities paralyzed in fear, Trish did the only thing she could. She screamed.

The second she opened her mouth, Rose lost her smile and snapped her head back into a normal position. Seconds later, voices could be heard. Her friends were coming to see what was happening.

"Take it," said Rose, stretching her hand towards Trish, "just take it." Her voice sounded childish once again.

"Enough," said the man, grabbing Rose's hand.

At that moment, two of Trish's male friends came over. Rose and the man both immediately adopted friendly, normal-looking smiles.

"Is everything all right?" one of the guys asked.

"They, they…" Trish struggled to speak. "They…"

"Oh, we're lost as can be!" said the man with a British accent. He hadn't spoken like that when he talked to Trish. "We were just asking this young lady for directions to our hotel."

"No!" Trish screamed. "No! They wanted me to take that fucking orange and-" She was cut off by the man's laughter.

"You kids need to take it easy with all that alcohol," he said, looking at the stack of empty bottles by the fire.

"No, I saw this woman before and..."

"Hey, Trish, take it easy," said one of her friends, putting the blanket around her. "You probably just had a nightmare or something."

"No, you don't understand-"

"All right, well, we better get going," said the man, taking Rose's hand.

"Sorry about this," Trish's friend said, smiling. "Looks like she had a bit too much to drink."

And just like that, Rose and the man left. Trish spent the night crying out of fear and frustration, and got on a plane home the next day.

The last time Trish encountered Rose was one month before we met in Provincetown.

It'd been a year since the last horror with the orange, and Trish had found a way to move on after some time. She often flew on trans-Atlantic flights. Pay was good, but traveling and seeing different places was even better. After one of those flights, Hong Kong to Toronto, I believe, Trish and the rest of the crew headed to the hotel Air Canada had provided for them. She loved that part of her job the most, staying in luxury hotels and having the room to herself.

That night, she brought some alcohol from the plane and just laid in bed, drinking. She probably had one too many because she passed out with the TV on, something she never does. At about 5am, she heard a quiet knock on her door. Still drunk, she ignored it, but there was another knock. And another.

"Go away!" Trish yelled, hoping that the maid, or whoever it was, would go away.

She heard the knock again.

"God fucking damn it," Trish said, rolling out of the bed, "someone better be dead."

When she opened the door, she realized that the news about someone close to her dying would've been better. In front of her stood Rose.

You know how when you're drunk and then something shocking happens, you sometimes sober up immediately? That's what happened to Trish. The influence of five small Smirnoffs faded away instantly.

Rose stood there, smiling widely and rocking back and forth.

"What... what do you want from me?" Trish cried.

"Take it. Now. He will, too. And then it will all be complete. Transfer will, at least," Rose said, still rocking. Trish could sense some excitement in Rose's oddly young voice.

I'm not sure if it was just a defense mechanism or a moment of pure madness, but Trish grabbed the orange out of the woman's hand and threw it down the hallway.

"Get the fuck out of my life, you freak!" Trish screamed at her.

All this aggression did to Rose was make her lose her smile. She didn't even flinch.

"I'll see you two soon," she said calmly in an adult voice. It was the first time either of us heard her speak like a normal person (when it was just the two of us). Trish remembers being terrified by it because her voice sounded so serious, even threatening. Of course, at the time, Trish and I didn't know each other, and she had no idea who "you two" were in Rose's mind.

I sat on our bed, not believing what Trish was saying to me. I was literally speechless. A million different thoughts ran through my mind. How was it possible that the same person was stalking my girlfriend and me before we even met each other? On different continents, at that? Who was the man with Rose? And finally, what the fuck did they want from us?

6

Come On, Open

Let's step back for a second. Be honest, what would you have done in such a situation? Would you have called the police? Contacted your family? Moved away, hoping it'd take her another ten years to find you again? As I mentioned before, I see the world by the light of logic, and I believe (or used to) that everything can be explained with science. But at that moment, when Trish told me that the same woman who had once made my life hell was also following her, I was clueless. So I did what you would probably do as well: I called the police.

Since I live in a small town that has a population of only a few thousand people, I've gotten to know a few of the local cops. As soon as Trish woke up the next morning (I didn't sleep at all that night), I called my buddy at the station. Luckily, the police didn't laugh at my story, which I was afraid they might, but there wasn't much they could do, either. They said that no law had been broken in the U.S., but that if I got more proof of Rose following us, I could file a restraining order. They did, however, keep the Polaroid on file, in case things escalated.

After my disappointing trip to the local P.D., I decided to go back to Boston and look around the place where I saw Rose. I knew chances were I'd find nothing, but I still had to do it. Trish wasn't thrilled about the idea, but she sure as hell wasn't staying alone at home, so she unwillingly came with me. The street I saw Rose on was vibrant with people, but none of them were the devilish woman who was slowly ruining our lives. We spent the next couple of hours in the city, trying to occupy our minds with something other than the fucking orange and the woman who carried it.

We arrived back in Provincetown at around 6:30pm. Trish and I lived in a fairly large house with five other roommates. When we got into our front yard, we noticed that the front door was open. This wasn't such a big deal considering how many people went in and out of the house, but with our increasing paranoia, even that was a red flag.

As we slowly entered our home, we noticed our bedroom door was open. The front door not being closed was one thing, but we always, and I mean *always*, locked our bedroom when we left. I could feel Trish shaking next to me, and quite frankly, I wasn't doing too much better myself. I yelled a couple of "hellos" into the hallway, to no response. As we got closer, I heard music coming from my room. Knowing that there was only one way to see what was happening inside, I stepped towards the door, and stopped cold.

Our room was... changed. All of our pillows were placed on the dresser. All of our towels and white shirts were put on the bed. The bed was completely stripped of all the sheets, which were now lying on the floor. My laptop was on our bed, open and playing music. As I scanned the room for the intruder who did it, my eyes stopped at the middle of the floor. On the spread-out comforter that was on the floor laid two halves of an orange. Trish must've seen them at the same moment I did, because I heard a barely audible gasp right next to me. If there was any doubt before that moment, it was clear now. Rose was back in our lives.

We immediately called the police, and it being such a small town, they arrived only a few minutes later. They took our statements, scanned the house and neighborhood, and gave us their private numbers should we need them. I suppose they started believing us. They chuckled when I asked if they were going to fingerprint anything -apparently, forensics doesn't come to the tip of Cape Cod for anything less than a dead body. They left within an hour of our discovery, and we were alone once again. Well, alone with the orange.

At that point, I was worried more about Trish than anything else. She is an emotional person, and these events were taking a huge toll on her well-being. I knew that I had to get her out of that place as soon as possible. But before we could make any further plans, we had to clean our room.

Trish put herself in charge of putting all of the stuff back to the proper places, and I was to get rid of that damn piece of fruit. When I picked it up, I noticed something. The orange itself looked terribly rotten, and it appeared that it was peeled on one side. I saw a small piece of peel underneath it. The section of peel had two words carved into it. It said:

AAAJDE OTVORI

In Serbian, my native language, "ajde" means "come on" while "otvori" means "open." Now, why was "ajde" written with three A's? I don't know. Was that the message we were supposed to receive? Again, no idea. What did "Come on, open" mean? That was the strangest thing of all. As I tried to make sense of this text, I heard Trish behind me.

"Babe..." she whispered in a voice strained with the effort not to cry. "Babe."

I turned around and saw her looking at my laptop. At that moment, I realized that the music that had been playing since we discovered the break-in was the same song on repeat. The song was "Africa" by Toto. That is my all-time favorite song that I started loving as a little child. But that wasn't what Trish was trying to show to me. She was showing me a picture on my laptop. My desktop background was changed. On it was a photo of two women with two kids; one of the women resembled my mom. They seemed to be in some sort of park. Hell, I'll include the picture here:

"Who are these people?" Trish asked me.

"I have no idea," I shrugged, still holding the orange peel. "Hold on, let me get rid of this garbage."

I threw the rotten fruit in the trash and studied the picture some more. The park in the photograph seemed awfully familiar. I emailed the image to my mom, telling her to call me as soon as she woke up, and Trish and I spent the rest of the night talking.

At that point, I was certain it was some sort of cult that was following us. No other explanations made sense to me. Trish, coming from an Indian culture, leaned more towards the supernatural side for answers. She claimed that it was a demon that wanted something from us. In her mind, us taking the orange meant accepting the monster and thus becoming demons ourselves. I entertained her ideas, but there was no way I was going to believe in a supernatural entity chasing me across the globe, offering me a piece of rotten fruit.

At about 3am that night, my mother got on Skype (it was 9am in Montenegro). She said that it was she and I in the photograph. Next to us was my mother's best friend with her son. The park we were at is in Sarajevo, Bosnia, where we lived at the time. The troubling thing was, this was the first time she had seen this photo. She doesn't remember it ever being taken. My mom wanted to know how I got it, and despite my determination to keep my parents in the dark so they wouldn't stress about my problems 5,000 miles away from home, I had to tell her. I spoke for a good thirty minutes, not leaving many details out. I retold the stories of Rose following me in Montenegro, I mentioned Trish's encounters with her, and I finally explained the last incident in our room. My mom seemed absolutely stunned at the story as she didn't say a single word while I spoke.

"Rose... *my* Rose? From work?" she asked, looking like she didn't believe a damn thing I said.

"Mom, I already told you... Yes, *your* Rose. It's Rose."

"Is this one of your imagination things again?" she asked.

At that point, I knew I needed to involve Trish in the conversation. When I was a child, my imagination had run wild and I'd often come to my parents telling them there was a strange man under my bed or that the TV would turn on by itself. At this point, I was the boy who cried wolf.

"Mrs. Bogetic..." Trish sat down in front of the computer and spoke softly, "He's telling the truth."

Seeing my girlfriend with such devastation on her face, my mom started to believe my story.

Unfortunately, she only ever knew Rose as a nice, chatty person from work with whom she enjoyed spending time with. Even after some thinking, my mother couldn't remember Rose ever acting strange or even asking about me. All this Skype conversation did was make my parents worried sick. They were helpless, and by the time I was getting ready to hang up, my mother was in tears.

"Call your grandma," she said while sobbing, "maybe she'll know something."

After ending the talk with my parents, it was Trish's turn to talk to hers. Unfortunately, her conversation was equally unhelpful. Her mom and dad knew nothing more than what they already told her, and now they were worried as well. They invited us to stay with them in Canada, but I needed a visa to go there, and even if I didn't, I knew that leaving would only be a temporary solution to this painfully permanent problem.

After talking with our parents and each other all day, we had two definite plans: Trish needed to leave and stay with friends, and I needed to call my grandmother and see if she could help with any information. Both of those things turned out to be good decisions.

7

Grandma's Story

Trish's college roommate lived in Pennsylvania and had been dying to reconnect, so we saw this as the perfect opportunity for her to get away from the whole situation. Her health was getting progressively worse from the stress, and knowing that she couldn't be of much help in my search for answers, I talked her into visiting her friend for at least a week. She argued for a while but finally caved in when I told her that there was a good chance she'd encounter Rose again if she stayed. We decided not to tell anyone about Trish's whereabouts; I figured if we were being stalked, the less information that was available, the better it was for us. I made sure Trish got on her plane (a direct flight to Philly), and went back to our house. I got a text from my mom telling me that she had talked to my grandma, but that my grandmother knew nothing about Rose. I decided to call her anyways.

I've always had a good relationship with my grandma, Dana. I probably wouldn't be lying if I told you that I was the favorite of her four grandkids. I'd often call her and spend hours just talking about all kinds of things, from my insignificant problems to her memories of the good old days. When I called her that day, she sounded less energetic than usual.

"Hey, Grandma, it's Milos."

"Hey, kid. What's up?"

"Listen, I know Mom called you and explained what's going on, and she said you knew nothing, but I still wanted to ask if you've ever heard of this Rose woman."

After a few seconds of strange silence, she answered with a short and unconvincing, "No."

"Grandma, are you sure?" I asked, feeling that she wasn't telling me everything.

"Whatever that woman wants you to take, just refuse it and you'll be fine," she said, sounding very serious.

"Look, if you know something, please tell me," I begged.

We went back and forth for a good five more minutes, me trying to convince her to speak, and her stubbornly denying my pleas. It took me telling her that both Trish and I could be seriously hurt should the situation escalate for her to finally cave in.

This is the story she told me.

∞∞∞∞∞∞∞∞∞∞∞∞∞∞∞∞

My grandma was an extremely energetic child. She was never at home; all of her days would be spent outside in nature. Back in the day, parents felt comfortable letting their children run around freely. My grandmother had several places she loved playing in, but none more than down by the river near her house. On this one particular day, none of her friends were available to play, but Grandma decided to head to the river anyway. She did her thing there for a while: built sand castles, fished, all the things that 1930's kids did for fun. When it started getting dark outside, my grandma decided to head home. Suddenly, she heard her name being called quietly.

"Dana…"

She turned around and saw nothing. There was only one path, surrounded by forest, leading to the river, and no one was on it. Then she heard it again, only louder.

"Dana!"

Her first thought was that her friends finally showed up and were trying to mess with her. She ran down the road but couldn't find anyone. She decided to come back to the shore and see if her friends had decided to finally end the prank and show themselves. Then she saw him.

He was a man of an average height, probably 6'or so, dressed in a black suit with a white dress shirt underneath, and the kind of unobtrusive black hat that gentlemen wore in 1930. In his right hand, he carried a long cane. The strange thing was... he was standing in the water. There he was, a man in expensive business clothes, standing in ice-cold water that was up to his hips. He was smiling.

My grandmother, more amused than scared, decided to walk over and see what this strange man was doing. She walked up to the water, but stopped when the freezing wave touched her feet.

"Mister, did you call me?" she asked in her most polite, talking-to-grownups voice.

"I've got something for you, Dana," the man said while his smile became even wider.

"How'd you know my name?" responded my grandma, entertained by this strange man. She had already started thinking about how she'd tell the story to all her friends.

"Oh, we all know your name, Dana," said the man as he took a step towards her. The water was now at a level a little above his knees.

"Who is *we*?"

The man didn't answer. As predictable as it's getting, I have to tell you what the man did. Out of his oversized coat pocket, he pulled an orange.

"This is your present," he said, stretching his hand towards my grandma although she was still at least ten feet away.

My grandmother grew up in a decently wealthy family, and fruit was hardly a luxury, so the orange certainly didn't cause a "wow" factor with her.

"No thanks, Mister, I'm alright," she responded, slowly losing interest in this whole situation. "You can give it to someone else."

"Oh, no, Dana, this one is especially for you," he answered, tilting his head at such a steep angle that my grandma was sure his hat would fall into the water.

"No, thanks," she responded, slowly backing up. Even though she was an adventurous spirit, she started sensing something was wrong.

"You take it, you take it now," the man said, dropping the smile.

Now, you have to understand, my grandma has seen some shit in her life. She lived through World War II and the Bosnian War, yet she says that even now, the man's face that evening is the scariest thing she's ever seen. She was a young kid with a vivid imagination, but she swears that the man's eyes got much darker as he spoke those words. She turned and bolted. As she was about to disappear in the forest, she turned around to see if the man was coming after her.

He wasn't. He was still standing in the icy river, holding the orange. As she watched, the man put the orange back into his pocket, and then took a golden pocket watch out of his coat. He checked the time, looked up to the sky, as if he were checking the weather, and started walking away. Through the river, the water still past his knees, step by step, he walked away. That was enough for Grandma; she turned around and ran back to the safety of her home.

My grandmother didn't see him again for more than twenty years. She grew up, and the man from the river became only a distant childhood memory. She would sometimes tell the story to her friends, but everyone would disregard it as the product of a child's blossoming imagination. In time, Grandma convinced herself that's exactly what it was, a small kid letting her mind run wild.

In 1952, Grandma brought my mom into the world. My mom was her first child, and according to our customs, it was a huge deal for the whole family, even the extended one. Celebrations started on the very day she was born, although my grandma was kept in hospital for two more days for observation. Apparently, there were complications during the birth and doctors wanted to keep an eye on her.

On the second night in the hospital, the man in the black suit came back.

My grandmother had a room to herself. She was deeply asleep in her bed when a bright light woke her up. In horror movies, you see a flickering light with nobody around, only for the monster to jump at you from behind your back. Well, that didn't happen. As soon as Grandma's eyes adjusted to the light, she saw the man standing in the middle of the room. He wore the same black suit, now outdated by more than two decades. On his head was a '30's top hat, and in his left hand, he carried the same cane. His right hand was tucked in his pocket.

She said that a hundred thousand things ran through her mind, but she remained speechless at the scene in front of her. It's funny how, in situations like that, your brain casts around for all the information it can find, trying to make sense of things. I suppose it's an evolutionary tool to help us survive. My grandmother's brain was no match for the irrationality of the situation in her room, which I suppose was what left her speechless. And just as she gathered the courage to speak, she noticed something else; the man looked exactly the same as the day she met him, more than twenty years ago.

"You did well," the man said, smiling. He revealed his flawlessly white teeth that went along with his seemingly ageless face.

"What… what is it that you want from me?" she asked, pulling the blanket up to her chin, as if it had some sort of shielding power to protect her from this ageless man in black.

"You brought the right one, Dana," he spoke softly. He took a step towards her, making my grandmother pull the blanket even higher, up to her nose.

"Brought who, what are you… what do you want from me?" she begged.

"You only have to take this, and it will all be over, I promise you." He took another step towards her, pulling an orange out of his right pocket.

"Leave, or I'll scream, I swear," she said, shaking from adrenalin and fear.

Apparently, that answer wasn't what the man wanted to hear. He tilted his head to the left while his smile widened. Taking another step towards her, he stopped barely a foot away and spoke in a child-like voice, as if he were a young boy instead of a man in his forties.

"It would be better for all of you if you took it, Dana, it really would." The childish voice made him seem even more terrifying, though she hadn't thought that was possible a moment ago.

"Get out!" she screamed at him, causing him to lose the smile and step back.

"Fine. He'll take it then. He'll serve the transfer."

The man cocked his head back, adjusted his top hat, and walked to the door. Before he exited, he turned the light off in the room. My grandma was left alone in her bed, shaking, surrounded by nothing but darkness and fear.

She never told anyone about this incident, until that day when I begged her for help. My grandmother said that, at the time, she had no idea who the "he" was that the man was referring to.

After a few years of always looking over her shoulder, my grandmother let her guard down, although time seemed irrelevant to the man. More than twenty years had passed in between the first two incidents, but Grandma was only a human who wanted to forget, so she moved on.

In 1992, the man in black from forty years ago was the last thing on my grandmother's mind. The war in Bosnia had started and my grandfather and she were stuck in a city that was being demolished by military pawns led by greedy politicians. We were absolutely helpless; no supplies were allowed through the borders of Bosnia, and the only thing we could do was talk to them on the phone. It was rough, trying to carry on a conversation while the sounds of shots being fired and exploding bombs could be heard in the background. The food supply was limited (and that's a generous description), so people had to resort to different methods of survival.

I remember the story of my cat, Pipi. Pipi was only a kitten when we left Bosnia. We had my grandparents watch her. When the war started, Pipi's food portions went down to barely anything, which was exactly what my grandparents were living on as well. My kitty then took it upon herself to save the family. Every day, every single fucking day, Pipi would go out and hunt pigeons. She'd bring the dead birds back to my grandparents' apartment, proud of her contribution. And let me tell you, that little bit of meat is what kept them going through the roughest of times. All three of them. Going out was no option since snipers were shooting every person in the street, so Pipi remained their lifeline for quite some time. Funny how animals can feel shit like that.

I digress, but that's how bad it was in Bosnia; my grandparents relied on a kitten for food.

In 1993, oranges started appearing at my grandparents' front door rug. First, it was only one a month, then they started finding them more often, maybe once a week. And every time my grandma would find them, she'd throw them out. My grandfather was shocked at her behavior in times of extreme food shortage, and kept asking for a reason why she thought trashing perfectly fine fruit was justifiable. She refused to answer, and after a while, my grandpa gave up and got on board with throwing the oranges out, especially when they started showing up every single day. Then, one evening, they heard a knock on the door.

Knocking wasn't normally a bad sign. If military wanted to get in the apartment and murder the two of them, they'd do so by breaking in, not polite knocking. However, there had been an incident a few days before that started with a similar knock on their door. When they opened it, they saw four young soldiers with Muslim emblems on their uniforms. My grandparents were Serbian, which meant that, in that war, they were the enemy of Muslims. They were dragged out in front of their building and put up against the wall, ready for execution. Just as the soldiers were about to fire, Grandpa's old friend and neighbor, who was a Muslim army commander at the time, showed up, probably coming back from combat. In short, he told the guys to get the fuck out before he executed them instead of my grandparents. They got the message, apologized, and left. I suppose you could say that my grandpa and grandma were lucky on more than one occasion.

Anyway, when they heard the knock again, my grandparents just assumed that the soldiers had come back. Two years of being in the heart of a war used up all of their fear, so they calmly walked over to the door and opened it. It wasn't the Muslim military. It was the man. Only this time, a woman was next to him.

My grandma wasn't able to state with certainty if the man actually didn't age the last time she saw him. However, when he stood in front of her that night in '93, there wasn't a doubt in her mind - the man looked exactly the same as the first time she encountered him, more than fifty years ago. He wore the same damn suit paired with a top hat and a wooden cane. Next to him was an unusually pale woman with cherry-red lips and eyes that would pierce through your soul.

"Hello, Dana," said the woman, smiling, paying no attention to my grandfather standing next to her.

"What the fuck is this?" demanded my grandfather. Immediately, both the man and woman's smiles faded away, and their heads turned towards my grandpa.

"You may want to remain silent for this," the man said, his voice cold and threatening.

My grandfather has been tortured, starved, and shot at, but he claims that he never felt such fear as when the man addressed him. The man and the woman turned their heads back to my grandmother, the woman tilting her head slightly and smiling again.

"Where is he?" she asked in a childish voice that didn't belong to a woman of her age.

"Who? What do you want? Can't you see we have nothing?" responded my grandma in desperation. She was so drained of emotion from the years of shit she'd been through that the man and woman, at least for the moment, didn't scare her like they should have.

"Don't argue, tell us where he is," said Rose. She sounded like a child being denied a toy at the store.

"Where *who* is?" jumped in my grandpa, genuinely puzzled by the strange situation.

"Your grandson," answered the man. His voice was boyish but cold; my grandfather could feel the blood freeze in his veins.

"He's in Montenegro," Grandpa answered, too confused to think of lying. "Why?"

The strangers' grins widened to inhuman proportions. They looked at each other, then turned around, almost mechanically, and walked down the stairs in perfect synchronization.

"And don't ever come back!" screamed my grandma after them.

My grandparents quickly went to the balcony and watched the strange couple leave. The man and the woman walked down the street with bullets flying everywhere, appearing not to give a damn about the danger surrounding them. My grandma couldn't see that well, but she swears their heads were still tilted to the side, and they both still wore Cheshire Cat grins.

8

The Bike Trail

After this story, seemingly worthy of a low-budget Hollywood horror movie, I was even more lost. My grandmother didn't help much; all her memories did was increase the mystery and multiply the questions. I assumed that the woman who visited my grandmother was Rose. In a strange way, I was relieved that Trish and I weren't the only ones harassed, as crazy as it sounds. Being emotionally exhausted from overanalyzing the situation, I reached the point of not giving a fuck anymore. I could feel the stress build up in my body. How could I not? What human can go through something like this and stay perfectly sane?

With Trish out of town, I took a day off work to get myself together the best way I knew how. I got my bike and decided to go on a long trip that would hopefully clear my mind and sweat out some stress. I decided to do a long 50-mile route from Provincetown to a city called Hyannis. The weather forecast announced possible showers, so I left all of my electronics at home and took only my helmet and some money. Ten miles into cycling, I was feeling good, and I swear, even if it was just for one damn second, I forgot about oranges.

After 30 miles or so, I hit a bike trail that led directly to Hyannis. This was the homestretch, in my mind, because the bike trail was fairly flat and easy, so the last 20 miles wouldn't take long. That was a good thing because the weather was getting progressively worse; heavy fog had set in and I could smell the rain coming. Visibility on the trail was only about 5 feet at best, but that didn't matter because I was literally the only biker out there. I suppose that normal people don't do long ass trips on rainy days.

Halfway through the bike trail, I started noticing benches on the side. I'd been on this road several times before, but I had never noticed the benches. Either way, they were a good idea. The trail was long, and I guess everyone needs a break sometimes. About 7 miles into the trail, I thought I heard laughing. I squeezed my brakes and slid for a few feet on the slick trail before stopping and dismounting. I listened. Nothing. At that time, the fog was so thick, I couldn't see more than few feet ahead of me, and rain had started coming down. I listened some more. Still nothing.

At this point, you probably think I'm a fucking moron. Hey, I agree with you. Instead of staying at home, locked up and with a baseball bat in my hands, I decided to embark on this journey alone and with nothing but a couple of bucks in my pocket. I was simply calling for trouble. You have to try and understand my state of mind at the time, though. I was completely emotionally and mentally drained and reached the point of simply not giving a fuck. Or, at least, I thought so.

I got back on my bike and started pedaling. A few minutes later, I heard the laughter again. I immediately assumed the worst. Since I didn't know whether the noise was coming from ahead or behind me, I decided to keep going. Luckily, the fog cleared out a bit and visibility went up. A mile or so later, I saw a figure on a bench some hundred feet ahead. At that moment, a much louder, sinister laughter broke out, echoing through the area. I tried telling myself that it was just a biker who sat down to rest, but both you and I know that I wouldn't be writing this if that were the case.

As I approached the laughing man, I could see more clearly that he was no biker. He wore something black. A few pedal strokes later it became obvious that the man was wearing a suit. A black suit, in a very old-fashioned style. As shivers started climbing up my spine, I sped up. I switched to the highest gear and started pedaling Armstrong style. I never took my eyes off of him, though. I noticed that the man had a top hat on, but no cane, which gave me just a tiny bit of relief; *perhaps it's just a random person walking*, I lied to myself. When I got very close to him, I saw that his hands were lying empty in his lap, and there was no phone, newspaper, or any other entertainment around him that could possibly make him laugh. He was looking straight ahead of him, paying no attention to me.

As I biked past him, he started laughing very loudly again. His eyes remained focused on a spot straight ahead of him, and I wasn't sure why he was laughing, but I had a terrible feeling it was related to me. Not wanting to find out what this man's deal was, I kept on pedaling. When I got a good distance ahead, I turned around and saw that he hadn't moved an inch and was still staring somewhere in the distance.

I finally made it to Hyannis, cursing at myself for the stupidity of my actions. My plan was to get on a bus that would take me back to Provincetown, since 50 miles biked was more than enough for me. However, when I made it to the bus stop, I was in for an unpleasant surprise. The only two bike racks on the bus were already taken. The driver, who I assume had to deal with these situations before, denied my several pleas to let me inside the bus with the bike. He stated some policy violations and told me that if I biked to a mid-point between the two towns, I could catch another bus that'd take me home. This meant that I'd have to go back on the bike trail, at night at that. Since my brilliant plan was to take only a few bucks with me, neither a hotel nor a cab were options. Spending the night roaming around the unfamiliar city or biking back through the foggy road were the only two things I could do. Again, I'm a fucking moron, but I convinced myself that the man on the trail was perfectly normal and probably wouldn't be there when I returned. I decided to bike.

When I entered the bike path, my heartbeat involuntarily sped up. I just felt... uneasy. Knowing that I'd reached a point of no return, I shook my head and kept plowing through the fog. A mile or two on the road, I noticed something on the ground ahead. This was strange since the trail maintenance crew was more than diligent when cleaning the trash, and you could hardly see any garbage, especially on the path itself. I slowed down. The thing on the ground was a GI Joe action figure. It looked nearly new. I figured that some kid had dropped it while biking with his dad. I sat back on my bike and kept going. Another mile or so, I noticed something else lying on the ground. At that point, I knew something was wrong. No parent would let his or her kid litter that much. Getting closer to the thing, I recognized what it was. A basketball. Not just any basketball, a chess-themed basketball.

Now, when I was a kid, basketball was my whole life. I played it, watched it, practiced it, you know, lived it, basically. I was out-of-this-world excited when my city organized a basketball tournament. I gathered the best team I could find and had many sleepless nights replaying all possible scenarios in my head. When the game day arrived, we were notified that only two teams in our category had showed up, which meant that we'd be getting awards and gifts whether we won or lost. Apparently, my team wasn't as good as I dreamt it to be, so we got our asses kicked. Nice thing was, though, that we got to go to the sports store and choose an item up to a certain price. All of my friends chose jerseys, shoes, etc. My attention, however, was caught by a unique chessboard basketball. The ball had 64 squares on it, 32 black and 32 white. I've never seen something like that before, so at risk of being made fun of by my teammates, I chose that as my reward. The funny thing is, that ball was god-awfully designed, because playing with it for more than a few minutes would give me headaches. I guess that pattern was just not meant for a basketball. Since it was basically useless, and I still got made fun of for it, I decided to get rid of the ball. One day, on my way home, as I was crossing a bridge, I kicked it as hard as I could into the river and watched it float away.

Twelve years later, I was holding the exact same ball in my hands, five thousand miles away from that bridge.

Sometimes, when I'm under a great deal of stress (or fear), my legs start shaking. Well, at that moment, my legs wouldn't move. My arms gave up too, so I dropped the ball and watched it roll off the trail. Realizing that I could be in serious danger, I forced myself to start moving. Remember how I said that I had reached the point of not giving a fuck?

Well, apparently, finding the ball that my 15-year-old self had abandoned on the other side of the globe more than a decade ago did wonders. When I got back on the bike, my apathy was replaced by anger. I was furious. I wanted to hurt the people who were fucking with my life. I wanted to scream. Instead of all that, I started biking, using my anger to drive the pedals as hard as I could.

After a mile or so, I spotted another object on the path. When I got close, I realized it was just a piece of wet newspaper. Not believing in coincidences, I stopped and looked at it. It was a newspaper from the college town I played basketball in. On the front page were my picture and an article telling about my life. If finding the ball and a GI Joe figure (which I now assumed was a toy from my childhood that I didn't remember) wasn't enough, the newspaper article lying on the trail confirmed that this whole thing was about me.

I decided that I wouldn't stop for anything again. Pedaling like a maniac, I passed by several more objects.

An Iron Maiden shirt I bought for their concert in New Jersey 7 years ago.

A picture of my family in a broken picture frame.

A Bart Simpson keychain I used to carry around in elementary school.

At that point, I wasn't sure if my pulse was going wild because of the fear or cycling so fast. Probably a combination of both. And the faster I'd pedal, the more often I'd stumble upon objects. I wasn't even paying attention to them as I just wanted to get the fuck out of this foggy trail. Then, I saw a dead cat lying on the ground. It awfully resembled my kitten Pipi that I owned back when I was a kid. As I approached to look at the poor animal and see if, by some crazy fucking miracle, it was my kitty, I heard laughter again. Only this time, it was a young girl laughing. I looked up and saw a woman sitting on the bench not more than ten feet away from me. She wore a white dress. There was no doubt.

It was Rose.

For the second time that day, my legs nearly quit working. I don't know what I expected, really. Did I think it was just a coincidence that my childhood memories were spread across the bike trail? Did I not think it was related to the fucking woman with the orange? I don't know. But still, seeing Rose sitting there sent a wave of fear into my body. And then, the fear inside me was replaced by anger once again. I wanted to end this. I wanted to know why she was ruining my life. I wanted answers, and I was going to get them.

With bravery fueled by frustration, I walked slowly towards Rose. She was still calmly sitting on the bench, smiling with those damn bright red lips and looking at me with her head tilted to the side. I faltered slightly as she came into clear view and I could see that she hadn't aged at all in the ten years I hadn't seen her. Even that couldn't stop me, though.

"Sit," Rose ordered in my native language.

"No," I answered firmly, wanting to let her know that, this time, I wasn't fucking around.

"You've been a very stubborn boy, Milos."

I snapped.

"What in the fuck do you want from me?!" I screamed. The knot of fear and anger in my chest was expanding. "What possible reason can there be for all this shit? You're ruining my life!"

"No need to yell, Milos," she answered, smiling, unfazed.

"No, there *is* a need to yell! Do you realize what you've done to me? My life is being ruined by you crazy fucks."

"I only want you to take it," she said, picking up an orange that was resting next to her on the bench. "All of this could have been avoided if you would have just taken it."

"First, tell me what it means, then maybe I'll take it," I replied. "And tell me who that man is."

"I can't tell you just yet," Rose said. The contrast between her adult, almost formal phrasing and the childish voice she spoke in was eerie.

"Well, fuck you and your fucking orange, I'm not taking shit. And next time I see you, you're getting arrested.

77

I've had enough of this," I said, turning around to go get my bike.

Rose lost her smile. Her head snapped upright, and she spoke with an adult voice. "It's not your decision to make."

"Yeah? And what are you going to do about it? More oranges?" I demanded. "I'm not joking, the next time you try shit like this, you're going to jail."

She started laughing, but it was definitely not an amused laugh. It was cold and mocking, as if I'd said something incredibly simple-minded.

"You think the police can help? Or your friends?" she said derisively. I *did* think the police could help, but the amount of confidence in her voice had me suddenly worried.

"What in the world are you two? A cult?"

She laughed again. "No."

"Then what?"

"You have much to learn about us," she said, "but only after you take it."

"If the police can't help, then I'll call other people for help. I'll call a pr-" she cut me off.

"A priest? You think he can help?" She smiled widely, and then laughed again. "Why don't you call your little priest when you get home?"

By this time, I was almost certain I was dealing with something supernatural. I have always relied on logical, scientific answers to this strange world, and they had never failed me before, but I'd never experienced anything like this before either. Even though it was ridiculous, I was starting to think I was talking to some kind of demon.

I had no idea what Rose meant by *your priest,* but I wasn't going to get any answers from her. The night had slowly started settling in, and I wasn't going to get stuck on the trail with this possibly ageless demon. I got back on my bike and pedaled away from Rose, who never moved from the bench.

I got on the bus at the last moment and was a complete wreck during the ride home. When I got to my house, I opened a big bottle of Jack Daniels, sat in my chair, and tried to analyze it all. Nothing made sense, but I had a feeling that I should know about this priest she was talking about. I am far from a religious man, and the last time I was in a church was when I got baptized at the age of six back in Montenegro. I assumed that the priest who performed the baptism was the one Rose was talking about, so I gave my dad a call and asked him to go to the church and see if the man was still there.

9

The Baptism

I was baptized in Montenegro in a church called Ostrog. I am in no way a believer, but this church is truly amazing. During the Turkish occupation, my people tore the original Ostrog apart and carried it rock by rock to the top of the mountain to ensure that no Turkish soldier got to it. They then rebuilt the church at the top, making it a true miracle of architecture. If there is one place on earth where I feel something "spiritual," it's there.

When I was six, my dad decided to baptize me. Neither of my parents are or were particularly religious, but baptizing kids was a tradition in the Balkans, and my dad is a traditional guy. I remember him having to call ahead and schedule the baptism because of the extremely high demand for that particular ceremony. There were so many people trying to baptize their kids, I had to do it with several others in one take. I just wanted to get through it as soon as possible.

When we arrived at the church, there was already a line of kids waiting to get in and be washed clean from the sin of their ancestors. Finally, the priest, Father Srdjan, started letting us in. However, when my turn to walk in came, the priest stopped me.

"You, you can't go in," he said, grabbing and holding me by my shoulder. I didn't know what to say to that, but my dad quickly jumped in.

"What's the problem, Father Srdjan?" asked my dad, laying his hand on my other shoulder. I guess you could say I was being held by two fathers.

"I know you, my son," Father Srdjan said to my dad. "I baptized you long time ago, when my beard wasn't as grey as it is now."

Indeed, this same man did baptize my dad some twenty years ago. He had been the priest of this church for many years.

"But your son can't go in there," continued the father, pointing at the baptizing chapel.

"Why not?" Dad asked in a surprisingly respectful tone.

"I shouldn't tell you. It is better if you have him baptized elsewhere."

"But Father, this is the most sacred place of all," responded my dad.

"Son, I can't tell you much more. But I will say, you must baptize him. Don't dare not to."

They spoke for a few more minutes, and when my dad realized that he wasn't getting either answers or a baptism for me, he took my hand and we left.

"What the hell did you do?" Dad asked me in the car, looking angry. I suppose the first logical assumption was that I somehow messed things up. Maybe he thought I pissed behind the church and got caught or something.

"I was with you the whole time," I answered truthfully, which silenced him.

When we got home, my dad's phone rang. It was Father Srdjan. He wanted us to come back without any further explanation. Now, the ride to Ostrog was a good 35 minutes long, but apparently, my dad really wanted me soaked in the holy water, so we got back into his old Volkswagen and got on the road. When we arrived at the church grounds, the priest was waiting for us.

"I decided to baptize your son despite..." said Srdjan while stroking his beard and looking away into the distance.

"Despite what?" asked my dad.

"Never mind. Let's hurry."

So I walked in circles while the priest spoke prayers I didn't understand and sprayed me with holy water I didn't want. When it was all done, he shook my dad's hand and said, "Go now, and don't come back unless something strange happens."

I could tell that my dad wanted answers, but he was already irritated by the priest's strange behavior, so he just made a donation to thank him for the services, and we left. That was twenty years ago.

I needed to know what Rose meant by "my priest," so I begged my dad to go back to the church and see if the man who baptized me still worked there. After some talking into, my father finally caved in and went to Ostrog. Father Srdjan was still there, although retired. He now only lived on the premises. My dad said that the man was really unresponsive, but some convincing and a hefty donation made him open up.

I was baptized on February 13, 1992. One night, before the ceremony, "my" priest was handling his sheep at the field near the church. Back in the day, priests handled their own animals for food, not like today where they rock Cadillacs and iPhones. While working with the sheep, Father Srdjan noticed a dark figure in the distance. This was strange because the church premises had closed a few hours earlier and the rest of the clerical staff were already in their designated housing.

"Hello? Who is that?" he asked.

"Come, Father," answered a calm, womanly voice from the dark.

Srdjan thought maybe a sick person or a beggar had wandered on the premises looking for help. This wasn't all that uncommon. But as soon as he stepped towards the figure, he felt something "unholy", as he said. He claimed that the sheep started acting scared, and he wasn't doing much better.

"What is it that you want?" asked the priest in an aggressive, confident voice. He had a strong feeling that he wasn't dealing with a well-meaning individual, and he wanted to show that he wasn't afraid.

"Tomorrow," answered the voice, "tomorrow, a boy will come to your church. His name is Milos. You will not baptize him."

Srdjan told my father that, despite all of the unholy things he encountered in his life, including many exorcisms, he felt scared.

"You and your kind aren't welcome on God's ground," the priest said.

"My kind, Father?" asked the woman, stepping forward. Father said she looked white as a ghost, with eyes that gave away her lack of a soul. "And what would my kind be?"

"You demons."

She laughed.

"Demons? Father, I know you're a man of the cloth, but believing in demons? That demands a *lot* of faith."

"Leave, now!" yelled the priest, raising his golden crucifix towards her.

"Listen to me, you pitiful man, you don't know what you have here. You had better do as I say, or you will never sleep peacefully again."

Then, she turned around and left. Srdjan stood there for quite some time, shaking in fear for the first time in his life.

You know the rest of the story. He denied me the baptism at first, only to change his mind and do it. When my dad came to visit him twenty years later, he claimed that he couldn't deny one of God's children a way to Jesus.

The priest said that for two weeks after the ceremony, the woman would show up in his window every night. She wouldn't say a word; she would just stare at him with her head tilted to the left. Then, his sheep started dying. There were no signs of fighting or foul play, they'd just be found dead in the morning. Finally, the priest claimed that the number of exorcisms skyrocketed at the church.

Now, I believed everything Father Srdjan said to my dad up to that point. I think it's safe to assume that the woman who visited him was Rose. Sure, she may have come to his window to harass him for disobeying. And all right, she may have killed his sheep even. But exorcisms? As soon as my dad mentioned that, I told him that the man was being overly dramatic. My dad said that he thought that as well, until the priest showed him a VHS of one of the exorcisms. Apparently, the church had cameras installed to record every such ritual.

My dad says that there was this 13-year-old girl in the chapel, and the priest was saying all the prayers. But when he sprayed holy water on her, she started talking nonsense and walking in circles. Srdjan called for two guys from the staff to hold her down, but they couldn't. Dad said that it was surreal watching a little girl dragging two large guys across the chapel.

My father was overwhelmed with all the information, and he wasn't sure what to believe. He wanted to leave, but he needed to find out who the woman was. Srdjan claimed that he initially thought that the woman was a demon, but her lack of fear when he prayed and her freedom on the holy ground suggested differently. He then went on with theories of her being a part of a cult, or maybe even Morana, the goddess of death. He claimed that he still occasionally sees her, most often on February 13, the day he baptized me. This whole experience apparently made Father Srdjan lose faith in God, who he claims should've protected him, and he retired not too long after the woman started coming to him.

I personally took most of this story with a grain of salt, as did Dad. We couldn't really be sure how much of it was true and how much was a fabrication of an old, probably senile mind. One thing I was sure about though: my patience was running out.

Imagine the amount of information running through my brain at the moment. I had to be on a constant lookout for

Rose and her company. I had to try and figure out what she wanted from me. I had to dig into my and my family's history for answers, which only lead to more questions. I had to worry about Trish and her well-being. It was rough, man.

As my tolerance for stress ran dangerously low, I made a decision: The next time I saw Rose, I was going to take the fucking orange.

10

I Took It

Trish had returned from visiting her friend, and I could tell she looked much better. She had regained some color, her mood had gotten better, and she didn't appear as scared. I chose not to tell her about my baptism story or the bike trail incident since I didn't want her to worry over things she couldn't influence. I told her that my days went by uneventfully and that the whole horror was most likely over. I don't know if she could tell I was lying or not, but she accepted my words with a warm smile, and we had a joyful day together for the first time in two months, since the Rose events restarted.

You would expect my next sentence to start with "but," wouldn't you? Well, there wasn't a "but." As a matter of fact, the next day was even better than the previous one. I got a call from a company I applied to work for, and they told me that I had gotten the job. My first real world, grown-up job. The only thing better than getting a good job was getting a good job far away from Provincetown. The company was offering me a position in Atlanta, Georgia, more than 1,000 miles away from all this horror.

I probably broke some sort of record for accepting a job offer. I didn't even let the recruiter finish her presentation. I took the job, and I told them I was coming in two days.

For the first time in weeks, Trish and I were happy. Not only was I about to start a professional career (until this damn book gets made into a Hollywood blockbuster), but Trish and I were also getting the hell out of Massachusetts, where Rose and the man seemed to dwell.

While we were packing our bags, we discussed all the great things about our upcoming stress-free life. Nowhere in our plans did we mention a demonic, orange-carrying woman in a white dress. We rented a car, filled it with all of our belongings, and went down to the sweet south where we would only find oranges in grocery stores.

The actual trip, while long, was a hell of a lot of fun. We'd eat at different restaurants, sleep in cool hotels, you know, the good-old road trip kind of thing. When we finally arrived in Atlanta, we were exhausted but excited at the prospect of our new life. Trish's brother and his family live in that city, so we stayed with them until we were able to find a fitting apartment. We managed to find an amazing one bedroom flat that had everything we needed. Watching Trish sign the lease made me giggle like a little kid; she seemed so happy that, if a stranger would've looked at her, they would have never guessed she went through hell so recently.

Then came the time to move in. We only had about six suitcases worth of stuff, so we decided that I would carry them upstairs while Trish went shopping for basic supplies and groceries. The suitcases were in the building's lobby, and our apartment was on the first floor. I brought in the first two bags and left the door open so I didn't have to unlock it again. During the second trip up the stairs, one of the bags opened and a few of my things fell out. Tired and frustrated, I cursed and gathered all of my stuff and dragged the suitcases into the apartment. One more trip and I would be done. I brought the last two bags into the living room, took off my shoes, and grabbed a can of Coke. After the first sip, I dropped it.

In the middle of our naked, unfurnished floor sat an orange. Time froze around me, and the only two things that made it into my brain were the foaming noise of spilled soda and a fucking orange in the center of my living room. You know how, when you're in a plane that's taking off, your ears get clogged and you have to move your jaw to fix them? That's what happened. It seemed like everything around me blurred out and my whole focus was on that goddamn piece of fruit. Then the spilled Coke made it to my feet and threw me back into the reality.

Rose.

I turned around and right there, at the entrance of the apartment, stood Rose and the man in the black suit. If I were better at artistic descriptions, I would be able to portray that whole scene better.

I was standing in my socks that were now soaked with soda. Behind me, on the floor, was an orange and in front of me, the two people who stalked Trish, my grandmother, and me for our whole lives. They looked happy and confident.

Rose wore the same white dress and her skin was as pale as ever. Her head was tilted to the left and her arms were just dangling at her sides. There was one thing different about her, though; she didn't have any lipstick on, although her grin was still there. I suppose that, if you saw her on the street and you had no prior knowledge of her, you'd think nothing of her. Behind Rose stood a man in the black suit, the same man from the bike trail. He looked old and strict. His pupils were contracted to near-pinpoints, but his eyes still gave the impression of depth. On his head was an old-school top hat, and in his right hand, he held a long cane.

The wave of feelings that came to me was overwhelming. The first emotion was, of course, fear. My initial thought was to run. But where? They were standing at the only entrance. The follow up thought was to fight. But why? What would that accomplish? And could I even win? Then came the peace. The unexpected peace. I realized what I should've realized a long time ago. There was no escape. No matter how many times I changed towns, cities, countries, or even continents, they'd always find me. No matter how long I'd reject it, the orange would always be there for me to take it. I had a choice of being followed for the rest of my life, or accepting the damn orange and seeing what happened.

With no energy left to resist, I muttered, "If I take it... Will you tell me why?"

Rose smiled even wider than before. She looked over her shoulder to the man, who nodded slightly in approval. She looked back at me, then at the orange behind me.

"Alright," I said, defeated.

I walked over to that fucking thing lying on the floor. I got down on one knee and took a second to study the piece of fruit. It looked just like a regular orange, except that it was a bit rotten. This was it. I inhaled deeply, closed my eyes, and took the orange. I don't know what I expected, really. I guess I (and probably you) expected some sort of immediate reaction from the universe. I thought about this moment many times before it actually happened, and taking the orange was never so... uneventful in my head. It was unusually quiet. When I finally opened my eyes, I realized that I was just holding a piece of rotten fruit, nothing more and nothing less. I turned around and looked at Rose and the man.

Her head wasn't tilted anymore, and the man had taken his hat off.

They looked normal.

"Come in," I said, lowering myself into a seated position on the floor.

11

The Story of Her Holding an Orange

Rose looked over to the man once again, and after another approving nod from him, she slowly walked into the room and sat in the only chair in the apartment.

"What would you like to know?" she asked, smiling. She didn't speak in the unnaturally childish voice she had used before, but in her natural tone. I almost felt relieved.

"Everything," I answered, looking at the man who still stood at the door.

"Curious, aren't we?" she said in a friendly tone, "I'll try my best."

I am telling you the full story now, which I've pieced together from all of the information from both Rose and my grandmother's findings. This is the story of how Rose became the woman holding an orange.

∞∞∞∞∞∞∞∞∞∞∞∞∞∞∞∞∞

My great-grandfather Jovo was only eighteen when he met my great-grandma Anka in the early 1920's. It was one of those love-at-first-sight things and they got married only a few weeks later. Anka became pregnant with my grandmother Dana shortly after. My great-grandfather was an adventurer and a world traveler, and he would often go on long trips by himself. The arrival of the child, however, changed that. He was no longer able to embark on exotic journeys because money was tight and responsibilities were piling up. I suppose that every man reaches a point when he has to stop being a kid and start being a grownup. Jovo wanted to be both.

During the late 1920's in Bosnia, there was a huge craze for African safaris in Europe. For some reason, African countries heavily advertised their tourism and many, many people went on those trips. Prices were affordable - how often does a regular person get to go on a safari? So, when my great-grandpa heard an ad on the radio offering a special honeymoon discount for one of those trips to Kenya, he didn't think twice. After some persuading, Anka agreed to Jovo's spontaneous idea and soon they were packing. They even managed to talk Anka's parents into taking care of my grandma while they were on their trip to explore the exotic land of Kenya.

My great-grandparents had the time of their lives for the first few days in Nairobi. They'd go sightseeing, animal observing, flea market shopping, you name it. They even met a lovely local couple that lived in an apartment complex next to the hotel. The couple, husband Das and wife Chandi, were also new to Kenya since they had just moved there from India. Apparently, the four of them met at the grocery store and clicked immediately, spending the next few days together, doing all of the before mentioned activities.

Then my great-grandmother got sick from drinking some contaminated water. Her life wasn't in danger, but the stomach pain and vomiting left her completely unable to get out of the bed. She didn't want my great-granddad to miss out on his dream trip, so she made him go out and do activities without her. Jovo called up the Indian couple, but Das was at work. Chandi, his wife, however, was free for the evening and loved the idea of an afternoon activity. They decided to go sightseeing on the outskirts of Nairobi in the Kiambu province. I suppose my great-grandmother hadn't noticed the chemistry between Chandi and Jovo, so she encouraged this adventure wholeheartedly.

You can already tell where this is going... When Jovo and Chandi finally got to their destination, they had a blast. They saw all the nature that Kiambu had to offer, and then they decided to have a few cocktails at a local bar. We all know what alcohol does for our animal instincts, so it was no surprise that, by a few mango vodkas later, Jovo was thinking about Chandi in a wholly different light. He was surprised, though, at how little resistance she put up to his rusty flirting, since she was a traditional Indian woman, and adultery was unacceptable in her culture. One could go into deep analyses of why someone would risk it all for a quick fling, but we are all human, and we all make mistakes, so let's leave it at that.

One more glass of liquid courage was the final push they needed to decide to escape the eyes of their tour guide and find a secret spot to do what they shouldn't. They settled for a nearby deserted barn. I'd rather not go into tremendous detail about my great-grandfather's sexual adventures, but let's just say that it was… loud. They were both so lost in the wave of passion. About ten minutes into the act that some would call sin, Chandi looked up and saw a little girl staring at them from the attic. Shocked, she immediately covered herself with her torn dress and let a muffled scream out. My great-grandpa jumped up as well, trying his best to cover his indecency.

"Hey there…" he said quietly, "do you speak English?"

The little girl, looking frightened, turned and disappeared in the dark of the attic.

"Go get her!" Chandi screamed.

Jovo climbed the old broken ladder leading to the high attic, trying to catch the girl before she escaped. He didn't really know what he was going to do. It wasn't like the girl knew either of them, and the danger of this affair being revealed by the child was nearly zero. Still, in the heat of the situation, and at Chandi's shrill urging, he climbed into the attic looking for the little intruder. The attic was dark, so he lit up his old Zippo lighter, a gift from my great-grandma. He found the girl standing in the corner, shivering in fear.

"Hey there, don't be scared," he spoke as he moved slowly towards her. "Do you understand what I'm telling you?"

The girl didn't respond at all; she only kept shaking. My great-grandfather wanted the child to know that she was safe. Then he felt something in his coat pocket.

It was an orange he had brought on the trip for a snack. Thinking that offering the kid the piece of fruit would be a sign of good intentions, he stepped closer towards her.

As Jovo moved closer, the child attempted to run. The old attic floor was made of cheap wood and it couldn't take all that activity. As the girl moved, the floor cracked below her and she fell through it. Shocked and terrified, Jovo looked through the hole and saw the child lying on the ground in an unnatural position. Her legs were horribly twisted, and her neck was dangerously tilted to the left. Her eyes were still open, although she was unable to speak or move. A second later, Chandi screamed.

"You killed her!" she yelled as Jovo tried to get down without getting killed himself. "You fucking killed her!"

"Calm down, I didn't do anything," responded Jovo, kneeling next to the girl and feeling her pulse. She was still alive.

Chandi started crying.

"We need to call for help," she said through the tears. "The child is about to die!"

"Listen, Chandi," said my great-grandfather, grabbing the woman's shoulders to calm her down. "If we call someone, they will know. We'll get discovered and both of our marriages are fucked."

Chandi stopped crying as she looked up into Jovo's determined eyes.

"I will lose Anka and you'll lose Das over this. Is that what you want?"

"No…" was all Chandi managed to say.

"All right, let's go then. I'm sure someone will find the child, and she'll be just fine."

As they were about to leave, Jovo stopped.

"Hold on," he said, walking back to the girl.

He put the orange next to her.

"What are you doing?"

"When she wakes up, if she remembers all this, I just want her to remember that I meant no harm."

And just like that, the two people, whose only sin up until then was adultery, became monsters. They left the barn, leaving the horribly broken child behind to die alone.

They found the worried tour guide in front of the bar and told him that it was time to go.

Jovo and Chandi went back to their partners, forcing themselves to forget the biggest mistake of their lives.

Six days had passed since the incident, and Jovo hadn't been able to find any articles in the newspapers telling the story of a girl who died or was injured in an accident. *Such an incident would definitely make it to the papers,* Jovo thought, because the girl obviously belonged to a higher social class and was probably a daughter of someone important. He decided that he'd keep the secret forever, never revealing the atrocity he had committed in a deserted farm on the outskirts of Nairobi.

Anka had recovered from the stomach poisoning just in time to travel back to Bosnia. Jovo was very excited to get out of the country where he'd become a monster. His excitement wore off when he saw that their ride to the airport was the tour guide who led Chandi and him to the province of Kiambu. The guide gave no signs of knowing about the accident, so Jovo calmed down. About twenty minutes into the silent drive, a smile took over his face because he was nearly in the clear. Then, the tour guide spoke.

"Have you guys heard about the girl from Kiambu?"

Jovo's smile instantly disappeared, and he was unable to reply.

Anka, seeing her husband go quiet, responded. "No, what happened?"

"Well, apparently, some rich white girl fell of an old barn and nearly died."

"She is alive?" Jovo jumped in, fear and excitement vying in his tone. He wanted the girl to be alive, but he was still afraid that somehow his affair would be discovered.

The driver chuckled. "See, that's where it gets interesting…"

"What do you mean?" asked Anka.

"Well, this girl fell off the building's attic, right? Supposedly, she got horribly injured. We're talking broken legs, arms, ribs, and even neck."

"Oh my god," gasped Anka, looking at Jovo who was losing color in his face.

"But that's not the worst part," spoke the driver. "No, see, the girl had been lying there for hours until someone found her. The worst part is, she was completely awake the whole time. She was paralyzed, but she could feel the pain. Imagine having to feel your every broken bone for hours without the ability to move or even be able to do so much as scream."

"My god, how did her parents let her do that? Is she going to be alright?"

"Is she?" jumped in Jovo, torn by guilt.

"Nobody knows. Her parents called all the best doctors they could buy in Kenya. They even rented a private helicopter to bring the medics in. All of the doctors had the same answer for them - she wasn't going to make it. I'm not sure what exactly was killing her. Apparently, her internal organs were pierced by the broken bones, and since she was found so late after the accident, she had no chances."

"Poor child," whispered my great-grandmother.

"But that's not why I'm telling you this. Those kinds of things happen daily here. Listen to this; so her father refused to come to peace with the fact that his only child was going to die. He kept calling doctors outside Kenya, even America, but nobody would come after the initial diagnosis by the other doctors. Then he decided to go a different route."

"What route?" asked Jovo. He saw the airport approaching, but he wasn't going to leave without knowing what happened.

"One of the servants in their house suggested the father call a Voodoo priest. We have a lot of those in Kenya. I personally don't believe in magic or Voodoo, but I know people who swear by it. Anyway, the girl's father, cornered and with no options, agreed to this act of desperation. Some locals brought in the community priest who also happened to practice Voodoo."

"You're not going to tell me that the priest saved her, are you?" asked Anka skeptically.

"Well... he didn't. They told me that he spent the whole night saying prayers, sacrificing animals, all that crazy stuff they do. By the time the sun came up, the child looked as pale as a ghost, and it was obvious that she wouldn't live to see another sunrise."

"So, the kid died?" asked Jovo as the car pulled into the airport drop-off zone.

"No," responded the driver, pulling his E-brake. "So get this; it's 6am, the whole family is surrounding the girl, and the priest is getting ready to make the final sacrifice. Then, they hear a knock on the door. They thought it was another family member trying to join the ceremony. But it wasn't."

"Who was it?" asked Anka, as intrigued as Jovo.

"Are you sure you're not going to be late for the flight?" said the driver, chuckling.

"Just tell us, for god's sake, man," responded Jovo.

"All right, all right. They open the door, and a man is standing there. He's not any of the family members, and he's not a friend or a neighbor. He was dressed really well, black suit with a nice hat. The family thought he was one of the million doctors they had called. But the priest knew the man was no doctor. He immediately stopped his prayer and stood up. A Voodoo priest *never* stops his prayer. To the shock of the whole room, the priest just collected his things and said he had to leave. Without saying anything else, he ran out of the house. The injured girl's mother broke down and started weeping, while the father fell to his knees, realizing that his final hope just went away. Then the man spoke.

'Your child is going to be dead before tonight,' said this gentleman in a black suit.

'What do you want from us?' asked one of the kid's uncles. 'We know that.'

'I can help.'

The whole room stared at him in shock.

'How?' asked the father in disbelief.

'That is not important. The question is, do you want your child to remain in this world.'

'Of course, what kind of a ques–' the father began, but was cut off by the man.

'I can make her live. But you will never see her again.'

'What? Are you joking? Get out of here!' yelled someone from the girl's bedside.

'What do you say? Do you want me to leave?' asked the man, looking at the child's father straight in the eyes.

They say that every single person in the room became quiet. The tension was unbearable, and all eyes were on the girl's dad.

'I don't know who you are... But if you can save my child, do it. She's nearly dead already,' said the father, starting to cry.

'No!' screamed the mother, throwing herself over the sleeping child. 'I'm not letting her go!'

The family talked to the father for a little bit more, and then they silently started leaving the room. They had to drag the mother outside. Was it crazy that they were willing to let the child go with a complete stranger? Yes. But they said that they felt unusual confidence in the man's voice, and they had run out of options. Thirty minutes later, when the mother came back to the room, the only thing she found was an empty bed."

"And that's it?" asked Jovo.

"That's it."

"Who was the man?" demanded Anka.

"Wish I could tell you. In these parts of the world, people don't like to dig too far into the supernatural."

"We'll be late for the plane," said Jovo, wanting to get as far away as he could.

They unloaded the car, and as they were entering the terminal, Jovo turned around.

"Just out of curiosity," he said, "what was the girl's name?"

"I believe it was Rose."

12

The Aftermath

"That's it?" I asked, intrigued but unsatisfied.

"That's it," Rose answered, smiling. She spoke in a natural, adult voice.

"So you're telling me that you were born sometime in the 1920's?"

"Can't remember the date anymore but around that time, yes," she answered with a serious look on her face.

"You're fucking with me, aren't you?"

"Most of you people do funny things, you see. Everything that doesn't immediately seem natural to you, you immediately deem supernatural, and therefore, impossible. But think about this - what if all of this was perfectly natural in our world, and you just never knew it existed? If a miracle happens, does it stop being a miracle since it now exists?"

"So you being nearly a hundred years old, and that man being some sort of an ageless demon, devil, whatever, I should believe all that blindly?"

"Do as you will, Milos. Perhaps I am just a crazy person," Rose said, sounding saner than I wanted her to.

"You answered exactly none of my questions, though. What was the orange about? Who's the man?" I asked, turning towards the door.

The man still stood there, motionless. Rose turned to him as well. He shook his head as if to say that she had said enough.

"Well, I'm afraid that's all for now," Rose said, getting up. "But who knows, maybe we will meet again. Probably not, but you never know."

"No. That *isn't* all. What about the orange? What does that mean?" I asked, frustrated.

Rose took another look at the man, who was visibly losing patience.

"The orange sets me free."

"And what happens to me?" I begged.

"I would ruin it all if I told you now," Rose said, gesturing to the man. He was standing beside the door, his hand on the knob, watching us intently. "But I promise you will soon find out."

"That's all you've got for me after all this? All I needed to do was take the fucking thing and all of this would've stopped?" I asked in disbelief.

"I always asked only that you take it, Milos," she answered as she walked towards the door. "Be good to Trish now, alright?"

Trish.

"Why were you stalking her? How is she related to this?" I pleaded in my final attempt at finding out the truth.

"Chandi, your great-grandfather's lover?"

"That was her... great-grandmother?" I mumbled, feeling dizzy.

Rose just smiled at me. The man put the hat back on his head and turned around.

"Goodbye now," said Rose as she closed the door of my new apartment.

I sat on the floor, staring at the orange. A million different thoughts raced through my mind. Trish opening the door was what finally snapped me back into reality. I hid the orange behind my back.

"What are you doing? I thought you were going to unpack!" she said as she brought the grocery bags in.

"Yeah, sorry, I just dozed off. I'll get to it now," I answered. At that moment, I decided to keep the final Rose encounter a secret. No good would come from Trish knowing what happened. Fuck, I didn't even know what happened.

A few days after I took the orange, I called up my grandmother and told her everything. At first, she was shocked by my story. Then things started making more sense. She confirmed most of the details from Rose's tale; my grandmother had found her father's diary and had seen some entries about Chandi and the accident at the barn. But who would ever be able to relate those events to a woman who stalks people across the planet?

Apparently, Jovo passed away not too long after the trip to Kenya. The official cause of death was complications after his appendix burst.

When I finished the conversation with my grandma, I sat down and thought long and hard about all of it.

To start with, I honestly don't think that Rose and the man had something to do with my great-grandfather's death. Let's just assume, even for a second, that the man really did save Rose from certain death. And let's put our rationality to the side and adopt the idea that the man in a black suit was some sort of supernatural entity. What happened after he took Rose? Did he revive her, raise her, and teach her his ways? Was she dead when I spoke to her? And most importantly, what were their motives? I suppose revenge would be a logical assumption. And if they did want revenge, they couldn't get it since my great-granddad passed away before they caught up with him. Fine. But why not choose my older brother, my mother, or anyone else from my family? And why not hurt me? The only thing they ever wanted for me to do was take the orange. Perhaps Trish and I were the first generation of Jovo and Chandi's descendants that had a chance of getting together. Still, how did they manage to get us together? And why? A million fucking questions and very few answers.

Hey, I know how crazy the story is. I find it ridiculous myself. But let's be honest, who could possibly expect a rational ending to such an irrational stream of events?

Even to this day, I stick with logic and reason, despite the many things I can't explain. Trish and I being stalked across the planet before we even met each other? Me seeing my childhood dead cat on the bike trail? Rose finding us absolutely everywhere? I can't rationalize that. But if you ask me right now, I will still reject any idea of supernatural entities being involved. I just can't believe it; it goes against everything in me.

Maybe she was just a crazy woman. After all, Trish, my grandmother, and I never saw Rose together. Maybe they were all different women with similar attributes. Maybe it was some sort of cult.

I still have the orange. I'm not really sure why, but I still keep it on top of the kitchen cabinets, tucked in the back where Trish can't find it. It hasn't rotted any further. It's strange, but I don't feel ready to get rid of something that so nearly ruined our lives.

I don't know what it all meant. What I *do* know is that I've moved on with my life. Trish and I are now married and are as happy as can be.

As a matter of fact, we are expecting a child in a few months.

It's a girl.

The End

Made in the USA
Lexington, KY
28 September 2014